Girls
Know Best
2

For a free color catalog describing Gareth Stevens' list of high-quality books and multimedia programs, call 1-800-542-2595 (USA) or 1-800-461-9120 (Canada). Gareth Stevens Publishing's Fax: (414) 225-0377.

Library of Congress Cataloging-in-Publication Data

Girls know best 2: tips on life & fun stuff to do / written by girls just like you!; compiled by Marianne Monson-Burton; [introduction by Tara Lipinski].
    p. cm. — (Girls know best)
    Originally published: Hillsboro, OR: Beyond Words Pub., © 1998.
    Includes bibliographical references and index.
    Summary: More than forty girls from around the country write on issues ranging from redecorating bedrooms and overcoming shyness to analyzing dreams.
    ISBN 0-8368-2453-9 (lib. bdg.)
    1. Girls—Psychology—Juvenile literature.   2. Girls—Conduct of life—Juvenile literature.   3. Girls—Health and hygiene—Juvenile literature.
4. Girls—Life skills guides—Juvenile literature.   5. Interpersonal relations—Juvenile literature.   [1. Girls—Psychology.   2. Conduct of life.
3. Girls—Health and hygiene.   4. Life skills.   5. Interpersonal relations.
6. Children's writings.   7. Youth's writings.]   I. Monson-Burton,
Marianne, 1975-   .   II. Title: Girls know best 2.   III. Series.
HQ777.G58   1999
305.23—dc21   99-13984

This North American edition first published in 1999 by
Gareth Stevens Publishing
1555 North RiverCenter Drive, Suite 201
Milwaukee, WI 53212 USA

This edition © 1999 by Gareth Stevens, Inc. Original edition published in 1998 by Beyond Words Publishing, Inc., 20827 NW Cornell Road, Suite 500, Hillsboro, OR 97124. Original edition © 1998 by Beyond Words Publishing, Inc. Additional end matter © 1999 by Gareth Stevens, Inc.

Editors: Marianne Monson-Burton, Michelle Roehm, and Amanda Hornby
Cover design: Marci Doane
Interior design: Heather Serena Speight
Proofreader: Hilary Russell
Gareth Stevens series editor: Dorothy L. Gibbs

The information contained in this book is intended to be educational and not for diagnosis, prescription, or treatment of mental and/or physical health disorders, whatsoever. This information should not replace competent medical and/or psychological care. The authors and publishers are in no way liable for any use or misuse of the information.

Printed in the United States of America

1 2 3 4 5 6 7 8 9 03 02 01 00 99

Girls Know Best 2

Tips On Life & Fun Stuff To Do

Written by Girls Just Like You!

Compiled by Marianne Monson-Burton

Gareth Stevens Publishing
MILWAUKEE

Foreword

The *Girls Know Best* books started with a "Girl Writer Contest," sponsored by Beyond Words Publishing, Inc. in Hillsboro, Oregon, hoping to find one girl author to publish. With, however, over 600 amazing contest entries, 38 girl authors became overnight celebrities, and Beyond Words received letters from authors and readers across the country thanking them for allowing girls' voices to be heard.

Beyond Words knew that *Girls Know Best* couldn't stop there! The contest continued to find new topics. Again, more incredible entries were received than could possibly be used. Twenty new topics by 47 girl authors were compiled into *Girls Know Best 2: Tips On Life & Fun Stuff To Do*.

Holding the contest, choosing the winners, working with the girls, and editing the writing was a huge job for editor Marianne Monson-Burton. Thanks go to Michelle Roehm, Amanda Hornby, Mary McMahon, and Heidi Schmaltz for their dedicated help and support, as well as to the parents, families, friends, and teachers of the young authors for encouraging their dreams. Thanks, also, to Tara Lipinski for being such a great role model for girls everywhere and for sharing her experience.

Special thanks go to all the girls who entered the contest. Their writing was truly inspiring, and those who achieved their dreams of seeing their words in print are proof that girls just like you can make their dreams come true.

The *Girls Know Best* collections give girls the chance to unite and speak for themselves. *You* know best about being a girl today, so enter the "Girl Writer Contest." (See contest guidelines "Do You Want To Be an Author, Too?" and the "Potential Author Questionnaire" in the back of this book.) Live your passion and become whatever you want to be!

Table Of Contents

Introduction

Tara Lipinski, age 16

✄ Hobbies: *playing tennis, horseback riding, sewing, going to Disney World, figure skating* 📖 Favorite book: Gone With The Wind ✎ Favorite classes: *math and biology* 📖 Hero: *Mary Lou Retton* ❋ Dreams: *to enjoy life to the fullest, continually set and achieve new goals, and be able to share with others some of the happiness that I have found myself*

Young Dreams

I can remember watching the Olympics on TV with my parents when I was only 3 years old. As those great athletes stood on the podium with their country's flag raised behind them, I knew that I wanted to be up on that podium some day. So you see, going to the Olympics has been a dream I have had for as long as I can remember. Sometimes when we set big dreams for ourselves, other people tell us that we are shooting too high. I have learned that no dream is impossible and that there is no such thing as trying for too much happiness!

Early Beginnings

As a little girl, I loved flying around the rink in my roller skates. I roller-skated competitively and I loved making the crowd laugh and smile. When I was 6, one of my friends from roller-skating decided to switch to ice-skating instead. She told me how much fun it was and convinced me to try it out. My parents and I went together to the ice-skating rink that first time, and they were excited to see how I would do.

Well, I stepped onto the ice and it was horrible! I fell all over the place and I couldn't even stay on my feet! My parents decided to get hot chocolate and leave me for a while to "practice." When they came back 30 minutes later, I was swirling and dancing all over the ice! This story has always inspired me to keep trying when things get difficult. If I had given up after those first few bruises, I would never have known the exhilaration of figure skating that I love today.

Along the way, there were many other challenges and disappointments that I faced. Going into the Olympic games, I had many doubts because few people believed in my ability to win. I fought through these doubts and leaned upon my mother's constant support. I learned that every time I approach a challenge with a firm belief in myself and with the willingness to work my very hardest, I am able to rise above the problems and achieve my goal.

Go For The Gold

Accomplishing my dream of being on a podium with the U.S. flag above me and Olympic gold around my neck was such an amazing feeling! All the challenges, the hours of practice, and the sacrifices that I made were worth it because I reached my dream. If you have a goal, then my advice is: go for it! No matter who you are, how old you are, who tries to discourage you, or what odds are against you—you can do it.

If you love what you are doing and you believe in yourself, then just keep doing what you love. Set a goal for yourself and you can make it happen. I have always tried to have fun with my skating because I think you have to love the process. I love how free I feel on the ice and how I am able to express my feelings through the performance. If you love what you do, then no matter where it takes you, you are making yourself happy and changing the world.

Girl Power

You can see in *Girls Know Best 2* that as girls across the world we have a lot of power. These girl authors are proof that all of us can reach our dreams, whatever they may be. This book also shows what it means to be a girl in America today: there are hard things but there are great parts too! Being a girl brings a feeling of pride that comes with the knowledge that as girls we are pulling together and enjoying our independence. Have fun—enjoy yourself and life! Believe that you can do anything. If we stand together we can change the world!

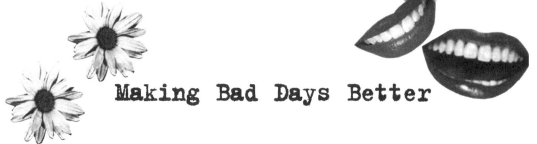

Making Bad Days Better

Allison Orsi, age 16 (left)

✄ Hobbies: *soccer, making soap, camping, singing, writing* ☺ Pet peeve: *misd speld wrods* ♫ Hero: *my dear, sweet mother* ❀ Dreams: *to hike the Chilkoot and travel around the world*

Tawnya Durand, age 16 (right)

✄ Hobbies: *kayaking, hiking, driving* ☺ Pet peeve: *sunshiny days when I have to be inside* ♫ Heroes: *Mother Teresa and my loving Mom* ❀ Dreams: *to be in the Iditarod, to have a strawberry farm and an exciting and enjoyable life*

Bad Day Blues

Everybody has a bad day sometimes. Maybe it's because you got a bad test score, got in an argument with a friend, or tripped down the stairs. Bad days do happen, but you shouldn't feel like there is nothing you can do about them. So when you are feeling down or blue, there is a way to start your day brand-spank'n-new! This chapter is full of sunshiny ideas and tips to make your day better and to help the people around you have better days, too.

Talking It Out

Sometimes talking about your day with a friend, parent, or teacher helps you let go of negative feelings.

Tawnya: My personal favorite way to deal with a bad day is to talk about my frustrations with a trustworthy friend. When I talk with a friend they might help me to see another point of view or offer some encouraging words. They might say, "Things will get better," or "I understand how you feel." Often all you need is a pal to cheer you up!

Writing It Out

Sometimes you may not feel like talking. That's okay! You can also let out your feelings by writing them down on paper. A journal can be a very useful friend to complain to. IMPORTANT TIP: If you are angry with someone and choose to write down how you feel, make sure the person you're angry with won't see your writing. If they see what you've written it will likely hurt their feelings or make them angry, too.

Letting Off Steam

If you really don't want to talk with anyone about your day and you don't want to write down how you're feeling, then don't just sit around and pity yourself. Self-pity is when you feel that everything is happening to you and there is nothing you can do to make your life better. It is important to know productive ways to let out your anger and frustration. If you are angry or upset, one way to let out tension is to pound your pillow. Pillows are soft, so if you hit them, you won't hurt yourself. Plus, pillows puff back up easily. Walks also can help you to think more clearly. Just getting your mind off of what you are angry about can give you a chance to cool down and see things in a different light.

Laughter Is Great Medicine

Laughing can make anybody feel better. Just pulling your face into a smile and letting out a giggle, hoot, snort, or peal of laughter can make you feel much better. If you are reading this chapter right now and are in need of a good laugh, grab a friend and have a contest to see who can come up with the corniest jokes!

Making sock puppets is a smashing activity that makes people smile and laugh. To make a sock puppet you need:

☞ An old clean sock (preferably one without a match)

☞ Markers for drawing a face on your sock

☞ Glue and construction paper for clothing and ears

☞ Yarn makes great hair (unless you prefer the bald sock puppet look)

Choose a fitting name for your sock (Sockly, Simon, Frank, George, Lucetta, Bert, or Milly are some examples of flattering names). Then you and some friends or siblings can put on a puppet show! This provides loads of fun and laughter—we know from experience!

Take Note

Allison: My personal favorite "cheer you up activity" is re-reading all the funny notes and letters that I have gotten from friends in the past. I have a special place where I keep all my old letters, just waiting for me when I need some sunshine. They make me smile and laugh when I read them.

Tawnya: Wow, Allison you're full of great advice!

Cheer-You-Up Activities

Now we would like to share some great activities that you can do to brighten up your bad days. Some of the activities are for yourself and some are for your friends and family. Try them out and see how much better you feel!

Spoil Yourself Royally

Sometimes doing special things for yourself can make a day much better. Here are seven ways to spoil yourself rotten!

1) Take a toasty warm bubble bath which will release the tension in your muscles.

2) Listen to some of your favorite music. Usually uplifting music can help to pull you out of a blue mood.

3) Re-read an old favorite book, or take a trip to the library to find something new. Two cheery books recommended by Allison and

Tawnya: *The Princess Bride*, by William Goldman and *Little House in the Big Woods*, by Laura Ingalls Wilder.

4) Go roller blading, biking, or on a walk with friends or by yourself. If you have a dog, they are great for grumpy days and would love to go with you.

5) Have a memory session! Remind yourself about fun things you have done with family members or friends. Pull out old photo albums and scrapbooks.

6) Doing something creative like painting a picture or making collages can be very delightful.

7) Drinking delicious tea will soothe your nerves, but if you are a chocolate lover like we are, cocoa is always satisfying, too!

Some of these ideas can be put together, like taking a bubble bath, drinking tea, and reading at the same time. But be careful not to drop your book in the bathtub!

A Special Box

Why not plan ahead for those *really* bad days? Do you have a special place where you keep the things that make you smile? If you don't, we suggest that you put a box together. You could decorate the box and then include photos or things that remind you of the happy times in life.

Every time something really great happens, tuck a note or memory from the event into your box. You could include a great report card, a blue ribbon from a swim meet, and a sweet note from a friend. There are so many good things in life that just need to be recognized. Here is a small list of things that make life wonderful: • Best friends • Picnics in the park • Puffy clouds • Sunny days • Chirping birds • Flowers • Fluffy snowflakes • Friendly smiles!

Happy Stripes For All

We invented this great thing called Happy Stripes. Happy Stripes are special strips of paper that friends can give to each other. Here is how you make Happy Stripes:

☺ First find a jar (medium-sized, washed-out salsa jars work great).

☺ Then think of all the terrific qualities that your friend has and write those qualities on small strips of paper.

☺ Next, stuff the strips of paper into your jar and screw the lid on.

☺ You can decorate the jar with ribbons, if you want.

When you're finished, hand the jar to your friend. The next time she has a bad day she can pull out a Happy Stripe and your compliment will brighten her day.

You could even have a Happy Stripe party! Make sure all your friends bring a jar, then have everyone sit in a circle. Each person writes something nice on a strip about every other person in the circle. Then you give the strip to the person it belongs to, and everyone leaves with their own jar of Happy Stripes!

Recovery Kits

A Recovery Kit is a box filled with fun stuff to do for someone who isn't feeling well. If your friend has just had her tonsils out or if she is recovering from itchy chicken pox, she would especially enjoy a Recovery Kit.

To make a Recovery Kit, you need an old shoe box to hold all the fun things. You can decorate the shoe box with cut-out pictures from magazines, glitter, construction paper, wrapping paper, yarn, bows, or stickers. You might choose to draw pictures on the shoe box using crayons, markers, colored pencils, or paint. After you are done decorating your recovery kit you need to decide what to put in it. Some ideas of what you can put in a recovery kit are: • Colorful stickers • A new box of crayons • A coloring book • Puzzles • Beads • A slinky • Cards to play "Old Maid" or "Go Fish" • Books for your friend to borrow or keep • Nail polish.

Keep Smiling

Well, we hope this chapter has made you feel much better and no longer blue. Although not every day is perfect, there are so many things you can do to improve them. We encourage you to use the advice given in this chapter. Remember, smile always and forever! Love, your chums, Allison and Tawnya.

Why I'm Just Like You

Anne Hopkins, age 13

✂ Hobbies: *singing, art, writing, acting* ☹ Pet peeve: *when people play with my wheelchair behind my back*

✄ Hero: *my mother* ❀ Dreams: *to help the world learn about people with disabilities and to be in a Broadway musical*

My Challenge

I am frequently asked, "Why are you in a wheelchair?" I don't mind this question; it's all right to ask me. Everyone is curious. I wanted to write this chapter to help girls understand me and other people with disabilities.

My brother Stevie and I have the disease SMA or Spinal Muscular Atrophy type II. This genetic disease affects the nerves in the spinal column. The nerves have trouble sending messages from the brain to the large muscles like my legs, arms, and back. Because of my condition, I am wheelchair-bound. I think of my wheels as my legs.

When I was a little girl, I never knew that I was different. I played house and slept with my dolly. I thought I was like the "other" kids. My playmates didn't care if their friends were disabled. We just wanted to have fun and accept everyone for their inside, instead of their outside.

I first realized that I was different when I became older. I started noticing the staring faces. Why was everyone looking at me? I could see the anxiety on the faces of people walking by me. They looked like they thought I was aiming my chair right at them. I'm happy to say I haven't killed anyone to date! Inside I felt the same as everyone else at the mall, the movies, in the grocery store, and the library. But I could hear people whispering about me from behind. I could hear little kids asking their parents, "Why is she in a wheelchair?" Of course the parents would say "Hush!" because they didn't want to be embarrassed. I wasn't angry with the children, but I was furious with the parents. I wished that they would let their kids talk to me and learn that I am a person, too.

Dos And Don'ts

I'm sure people wonder about how to act around the disabled and maybe you do, too. You may wonder if you're going to offend us or say something wrong. Here are some easy dos and don'ts to remember.

Do:

☞ treat us like you would treat anyone else.

☞ ask if you can help if we seem to be struggling. We do need help sometimes, so it's nice of people to ask.

☞ use the words "disabled" and "handicapped."

☞ act as if we're like anyone else and don't be afraid.

☞ look us in the eye, smile, and say "Hi."

☞ when in doubt, ask us what's appropriate—it shows you care.

Don't:

☞ constantly ask if we need help.

☞ talk really loud as if we're deaf when we're not—that's really annoying.

☞ put the disability in front of the person. Instead of saying "disabled kids," say "kids with disabilities."

☞ ever use words like "crippled" and "vegetable." These words offend us and make it sound as if we are not alive.

☞ ignore us and pretend we don't exist.

Growing Up

You may not know this, but at the age of 3 all children with disabilities attend early education programs with other children with disabilities. At age 5, I was mainstreamed into kindergarten as a result of laws protecting the handicapped. Even with this new law I couldn't go to the grade school in my neighborhood. I had an hour long bus ride every day to and from school. When my family moved to a new home, the laws changed once again. This law made the school district send me to my closest school. I got to go to class with the kids in my own neighborhood. I liked this better because I could play with my new friends after school and attend various activities such as art club.

Laws = Freedom

I am so glad that America has laws to protect the disabled. In some countries people with disabilities are considered outcasts. In America, laws help us get into places and receive fair opportunities. I am glad that there were people ahead of me who have fought for the Americans with Disabilities Act (ADA). It has made my life a lot easier. This law says that all public places must be handicap-accessible unless they are old buildings. That means they have to have ramps as well as stairs and doors wide enough for wheelchairs to fit through. If old buildings are remodeled, they must follow the ADA law. If I didn't receive help through these present laws, I would never have met the friends I have and I would still be attending a school far from my home; I would be miserable. But instead, now I'm a really happy and bubbly teenager.

Frustrations

There are definitely some down-sides to being in a wheelchair. Some places aren't wheelchair accessible, and I can't enter. I really become upset when this happens because we drive out to eat some-where, and it's not handicap-accessible. Then they tell us they can lift our wheelchairs. Yeah right! My wheelchair alone weighs 300 pounds!

It is also frustrating when I go to the store and I can't get through because of the things lying around in the aisles. When people are in the way, I say "Excuse me," but sometimes they don't move. Maybe they don't hear me, or maybe they just ignore me. Riding down the halls in school I face the same problem: students won't move. Students walk backwards and they run into me or have their toes run over.

In the spring and summer, I go on bike rides with my family and friends. Sometimes I wish I could ride a bike or roller blade, but I can't. When people get on a bike or step into their roller blades, they don't think that other people can't do what they do every day.

A lot of people in the world take things for granted. Even getting a glass of water or picking something up from the ground can be a challenge for me. Sometimes I make up contraptions to do these things. Usually it's a long spoon with a rolled up piece of tape on it. As you can see, being in a wheelchair isn't all that luxurious!

Life At School

I like school a lot. If we didn't have school, I would be bored out of my mind. A lot of people help me out at school, especially my aide Mrs. Campbell. She's been with me since sixth grade and we have grown close. Every day she waits for me to come off the bus and she takes my books out of my backpack. Mrs. Campbell is there to help me with the things I cannot do on my own. When my hands become too weak to write, I dictate what I want on the paper, and she writes it down. She helps me to prepare for things such as labs in science and hands-on activities. She's my mom away from home!

Just like everyone else, when I am at school I need to move around and stretch. Everyday they lift me out of my chair to exercise my arms and legs so I can stay strong. I guess you could call this my gym class. I go to occupational and physical therapy at school. These therapies are very important to my health, and they make my body feel good.

Boy Craze

Some parts of my middle school life have been hard. I've started to notice boys, and my emotions have been bouncing off the walls. I am sad sometimes because it feels like everyone has a boyfriend except me.

Sometimes I wonder if they're scared that their friends won't think it's cool to go out with a "wheelchair girl." One time I remember I was at a dance and one of my friends was asked to dance two times by two different guys. I was sitting right there, watching and waiting. I felt so sad, like tears were going to rush out of my eyes. Even people in wheelchairs can be wallflowers. All teenage girls have problems in their teen years and I'm not any different. But I will get through it and I know people will be there for me.

Right now my friends are a very important part of my life. I need friends for a shoulder to cry on, gossip updates, and for good heart-to-heart laughs. I have many friends and I love them. We go to movies, the mall, have sleepovers, and talk on the phone for hours. They help me and I help them. When they are tired of walking, they hop on the back of my wheelchair for a ride. People might think it looks a little weird, but we like it.

Interviews With My Friends

My friends are very honest with me. I asked them a few questions about being friends with me, and this is what they said:

How did you feel when we first met?
Jessica: I felt normal, just like anyone else feels when they meet their best friend: hopeful, happy, curious, excited.
Renee: I was unsure how to act around Annie. I didn't want to offend her by offering to do things that she could do or didn't want help with.
Vanessa: I was kind of scared when I met Annie because I didn't know what to say and what not to say.

What most annoys you about being out in public?
Jessica: It annoys me when people whisper and stare, or when people say, "Oh cool a wheelchair! How fast does it go?"

Renee: I don't like it when people stare, whisper, and point.

Vanessa: I hate it when people stare!

How do you deal with these people?

Jessica: I just ignore them because I know Annie and don't think Annie is different.

Renee: I give them the "look."

Vanessa: I try to ignore them and forget about it.

Annie: My friends and I try to ignore what people do in public places because if we didn't, there wouldn't be any time left for fun.

Just For Fun

Sometimes people underestimate how much fun people can have, in spite of their disabilities. For instance, my brother Stevie really wanted to play baseball when he was little and didn't understand why he couldn't play with everyone else on the baseball teams. My mom knew what to do and pushed for the first disabled baseball league in our town. Now I play on the team, too! For every game we bring a buddy who helps us retrieve the ball. I love going to the field and seeing the kids and their smiling faces when they hit the ball and make it to home base. My mom has also started a handicapped bowling league. I used to attend a Tae Kwon Do class. It was fun and I even broke a board!

My ultimate favorite activity is swimming. I love the water because I'm free from my wheelchair. It almost feels as though I'm walking. When I was little, my parents couldn't coax me out of the water, even if the water was ice cold. They called me their "fish." I used to swim through hoops and people's legs. Now I can even perform a frontward flip, with the help of my mom!

I find it amazing that many people assume I can't do very much because of my disability. I have done my best to prove that this is not so. I have performed in talent shows, had a lead part in the school play, and played many sports. But sometimes people still assume we can't do things. One time when my brother and my mom were at a restaurant the waitress asked my mom, "Should I give him a menu? Can he read?" My mom told my brother to order, and he said, "Why should I? They already think I can't talk!" My mom felt so sorry for him. I know that Stevie felt really angry. I believe that people with disabilities should tell other people, "I can do this," and not give up on themselves. Then other people will understand that we can do many things.

My Hopes And Dreams

I know the cure for my disease will come someday because of all the genetic research being done. I'm grateful for the medical professionals who help people suffering from my disease. When I grow up, I would like to be a social worker and help children with family problems and maybe even help teenagers who are disabled and are going through the same problems that I'm facing now. I would also like to be a scientist and find the cure for my disease, SMA. That would help many people. I think it would be exciting to travel across America and speak to big groups about the disabled. I know when the time comes that I'll know what to do with my life, but until then my mind can travel as far as it wants to.

Dreams only come if you work at them. I know that there are many things in life to learn and do. Life is just too precious to let it slip away. You have to take what you have and make the best out of it!

How To Have The GREATEST Slumber Party Of All Time

Stephanie Balshaw, age 11
✂ Hobbies: *tennis, shopping, reading* ❀ Dream: *to be a teacher*

Alyssa Lott, age 10
✂ Hobbies: *reading, playing with pets and friends* ❀ Dream: *to do something courageous and heartfelt*

Caitlin Davies, age 11
✂ Hobbies: *soccer, ice-skating, piano, dance* ❀ Dream: *to be the first woman on Mars* ♫ Hero: *Tara Lipinski*

Libby Hazzard, age 10
✂ Hobbies: *reading, swimming, soccer* ❀ Dream: *to be a teacher*

Colleen Mitchell, age 10
✂ Hobbies: *horseback riding, reading, writing, roller blading* ❀ Dream: *to be a famous actress or author*

We are going to teach you how to have the greatest slumber party of all time. We chose this topic because sleepovers happen often, so new ideas are always helpful. It is also good to have some advice, because anything can happen at a sleepover.

The Main Ingredients

There are certain ingredients you must have for a great sleepover.
1) Be sure to invite your best friends. We suggest a maximum of eight girls. Keep it an even number of people at the party so no one gets

left out. Make sure to think about how your friends get along, and who will feel badly if you don't ask them.

2) Pick a room in your house where you can have fun without disturbing your family.

3) Make sure you have plenty of food to eat. Don't forget to keep some food hidden for late night snacks.

4) Decide what activities or games you want to play, and plan ahead. See the end of this chapter for party theme ideas.

What To Bring

It is very important to bring the right stuff. Most importantly, bring yourself, ready to rock and roll! Don't forget: • A sleeping bag • Pillow • Pajamas • Extra change of clothes • Toothbrush.

Optional: • Stuffed animal • Nail polish • Tapes • CDs. It's fun to bring extras, but don't bring your whole room, because there will be lots to do! Here are some great games you can play.

The Greatest Party Games

Tanya Collings, age 12

❀ Dream: *to be a science fiction writer*

M&M Master

Materials: A cookie sheet, one straw for each person, a sack of M&Ms, one bowl for each player.

How to play: Spread the M&Ms on a large cookie sheet. Place an empty bowl next to each player and give them each a straw. At the count of three all the players attempt to suck the most M&Ms into their bowl. To do this, you place one end of the straw on an M&M and the *other* end in your mouth. Now suck in and the straw is like a vacuum cleaner. When the game begins, everyone tries to move as many M&Ms as possible into their own bowl. The player with the most M&Ms when 3 minutes are up is the ultimate M&M master!

Hanging Doughnuts

Materials: A box of doughnuts, string, and several doughnut lovers.

How to play: Hang the doughnuts (one for each player) by string somewhere in your house. A hanging pan rack in your kitchen works great. Make sure that the doughnuts reach down to each player's chin. The winner of this game is the first one to eat their doughnut without using their hands! Make sure you put a tablecloth down on the floor--it can get very messy!

Blind Makeover

Materials: A blindfold, makeup, and a mirror. (Hint: don't use mascara or anything that might hurt your eyes.)

How to play: Have everyone sit in a circle. Pick two extremely brave girls to sit in the middle of the circle. Blindfold one of them and have her apply the makeup to her partner's face. The girl receiving the makeover is not allowed to look in the mirror until all are finished. Every girl takes a turn getting her "makeover." When everyone has had a turn, they can look in the mirror. (Caution: this may result in sudden laughter!)

Rainbow Nails

Materials: 10 to 20 bottles of fingernail polish and a mustard bottle or anything else you can spin.

How to play: Have everyone sit in a circle. Place the fingernail polish bottles in a smaller circle with a few bottles in front of each girl. Lay the mustard bottle on its side in the middle of the circle. Everyone takes a turn spinning the bottle. When the bottle stops, paint one fingernail or toenail with whatever color polish the bottle points to. Continue doing this until everyone has painted all their nails in an interesting array of colors!

What's My Name?

Materials: Before your friends come, make a sticker for each guest that has the name of some famous person. If you have a theme for the party, then make them fit your theme. For instance, for a "B" party you could use Beverly Cleary, Betty Boop, Bill Clinton, Bill Cosby, and Betty Crocker.

How To Play: When your friends come, stick one name on everyone's back. Don't let them read the name, though! Then everyone has to discover their new identity by asking other people in the room yes-or-no questions about their character!

Other Activities

If you get tired of games, you can still have lots of fun. We especially like going out as a group. You could see a movie, go bowling, ice skating, or miniature golfing. Renting a movie is always popular. Don't ask your parents to take you to too many places, though, or they will probably get frustrated.

Getting Ready For Bed

Getting ready for bed can be a huge ordeal. First you have to decide where you are going to sleep. Then you all change into your pajamas. After brushing your teeth, get settled in and prepare for staying up late.

Midnight Madness

This is the silly, crazy, downright dirty fun of sleepovers! We especially like staying up late for good old-fashioned girl talk. This is where you pull out all the food you saved for late night snacks. It is also fun, once you are in your sleeping bags, to take out your class pictures and pair up the boys and girls in couples. We recommend that you go to bed before 3:00 a.m. so that you aren't too grumpy the next morning. Sometimes it is fun to set records to see who can stay up the longest.

Late Night Tricks

If you do stay up really late, you might want to play tricks on the people who fall asleep early. Don't play tricks that are really mean, though. You don't want people to cry or tell their parents or anything. Here are some harmless tricks to play on the early dozers.

1) Spread toothpaste on the person's feet. They will be in for quite a surprise when they wake up!

2) This one requires a marker (preferably a washable one!). You write the name of a boy that the girl likes on her forehead. For example: Mary + Matt.

3) Get your dad's shaving cream and spray it on your friend's hand. Then tickle her face, and to stop the tickling she will wipe her face with the shaving cream! (Make sure you don't get near her eyes, though.)

If You Get The Blues

It is hard to be at a sleepover if you feel left out. Try not to be sulky or whiny, because people might think you're babyish. If you're in a fight with someone there, don't make other people join sides. That will only annoy people and make the hostess feel like the party is ruined. If you feel like you're going solo and not hanging out with the others, here are some tips:

1) Get their attention. Tell a funny joke, do a funny dance—just do *something*!

2) If one person is being snotty, talk to someone else. The tension will probably disappear.

3) Suggest a game or activity where everyone can feel involved.

4) If it is really bad, then confess. Tell folks at the party that you feel like you are left out. Then they might make an effort to get you in the group. If you notice someone else is feeling left out, make a special effort to be kind and friendly.

Marvelous Morning

Just because it is morning doesn't mean the party is over. There is still lots of fun to have and another meal to share in the A.M. After you get up, the whole party can make breakfast. You should get packed up so that you are ready to roll when your parents arrive. After breakfast you can play any games that you didn't get to play the night before or that you would like to play again. You could even go outside and play a game like tag. Enjoy your last few minutes together! For some final advice, we called in two experts for some cool party theme ideas.

 ## The Greatest Party Themes

Kelsi Okuda, age 10
❀ Dream: *to go to the Olympics in swimming*

Katie Clarke, age 12
❀ Dream: *to be a kindergarten teacher*

The best parties are the wackiest ones, and choosing a theme is always a great way to liven up your party. There are lots of things in life to celebrate! You could throw a party to celebrate the first day of spring, the last day of school, losing teeth, or even the weather. If it has been a really long, cold winter, then have an "I'm sick of winter" party! Turn up the heat, have all your friends wear shorts, serve lemonade, and play summer games like nerf volleyball or croquet! Here are some of our favorite party themes—but don't forget to be creative and dream up your own.

Awesome Alphabet

Celebrate the letters of the alphabet! Let's take the letter B for example. Why the letter B? Because balloons, babies, and brownies are just a few of the reasons to celebrate the letter B.

ℬ Liven up your invitations with stickers of things that start with B: bees, butterflies, bears. ℬ Decorate with blue balloons, baby's breath, and buttercups. ℬ Have your friends bring baby pictures and guess who is who! ℬ Make sure you have plenty of bubbles and bubble gum. It's time for a bubble contest! ℬ See who can write down the most "B" words in 5 minutes. ℬ For food, serve burgers, beans, barbecue chips, berry flavored jello, bug juice, and brownies.

This is just the letter B and there are 25 more letters you can party with!

Ride The Rage

It is always fun to throw a party and celebrate whatever you and your friends are really into. Whether you love stickers, candles, incense, Beanie Babies™, or the new movie that's out, you are sure to have a good time with this theme. For instance, if all your friends collect Beanie Babies™, have a party where everyone brings their favorite baby. For a game, have each guest make up a new Beanie Baby™, name it, and design how it looks.

Time To Get Artsy!

Here's a theme for the artists among us! Even if you don't feel really artistic, everyone can have a great time making stationary with rubber stamps. You could also give guests a white pillowcase to decorate with stencils and puff paint. For dinner,

give each friend a piece of pizza dough, lay out toppings and sauce, create a "picture," bake, and enjoy!

Your Own Olympics

Are you into sports? You can organize your own Olympics! Have each guest represent a different country, and make their own flag. Then let the games begin! You could play basketball, have a gymnastics competition (use a folded blanket for a balance beam or vault), have a soccer tournament (doorways work as goals). If you have a local pool, you could include wacky relay races.

Add A Little Color

This theme is great for people who love colors. To have a rainbow party, ask your friends to each wear a different color. At the party, you could make friendship bracelets with colorful yarn. For food, serve rainbow jello! If you like party favors, give your guests a mini-prism to take home.

If you follow these theme party guidelines, you have all the ingredients for a fabulous night!

Working Girls

Clare Barnett, age 12

✂ Hobbies: *horseback riding, writing, reading* ☺ Pet peeve: *when my mom tells me to clean my room* ❀ Dream: *that all nuclear weapons will be destroyed one day*

Emily Nelson, age 13

✂ Hobby: *basketball* ☺ Pet peeve: *people who don't act like themselves just to be popular* ♫ Heroes: *my sisters and my mom* ❀ Dream: *to be the best person I can be*

We decided to write this chapter because we've tried many different ways to start a business. Now we both have jobs that we really enjoy, but we went through a lot of trial and error, and we'd like to share what we learned. It's hard to get a business started unless you have a clear plan of what you're doing. That's why we're here. As girls, we don't have to wing it when it comes to starting our own businesses. We all have the ability to achieve our dreams. We hope our suggestions help, but don't let them limit your ideas. Be creative and don't forget: it's *you* that makes the business.

Why Start Working?

Obviously, one reason girls work is for the money, but working should also be enjoyable. You don't have to love every minute, but you won't be happy if you hate the job. Choose your job based on what you like to do. Also, choose a job that fits your schedule and the amount of time you have to spend.

Clare: Since I want to be a veterinarian when I grow up, I thought it would be good experience to work with animals. Now I do pet-sitting in my neighborhood.

Emily: I like to do a variety of things and have lots of different experiences. So I do odd jobs for my neighbors and I have a great time!

Some Jobs To Consider

If you need help choosing a job, remember that there are endless possibilities! Here are only a few to consider. Choose according to your personality.

Are You A People Person?

$ Baby-sitting: Do you like kids? Do you feel comfortable being in charge? Start your own baby-sitting service.

$ Kid's Camp Counselor: Are you overflowing with energy and creative ideas? If so, hold a summer camp for kids in your neighborhood.

$ Kid's Party Organizer: Are you always the life of the party? Are you good at entertaining little kids? Plan and help parents out at kids' birthday parties!

$ Errand Girl: Are you a fast, efficient shopper? Run errands and do shopping for busy people in your neighborhood.

$ Tutor: Are you an ace in school? Can you help little kids understand their lessons? Start your own tutoring service for kids at elementary schools.

Are You An Animal Lover?

$ Dog Washer: Are you willing to get soapy with dogs? You could open your own neighborhood dog washing or grooming business.

$ Dog Walker: Are you up for some exercise? Become a professional dog walker.

$ Pet-sitter: If you love animals and are willing to walk, feed, groom, and play with pets while their owners are away, this is the job for you.

Are You A Creative Soul?

$ Selling Crafts: Do you enjoy expressing yourself and creating art? Try selling your creations.

$ Paint T-Shirts: Are you a Picasso when it comes to cool designs? Start selling your awesome clothing.

$ Room Redecorator: Does your sense of style rock? Is your room the definition of cool? Ask friends and relatives if their room could use a makeover.

$ Gift Basket Designer: Do you know how to put together a cool gift basket? Can you afford the money for supplies? If so, make and sell baskets for every occasion.

$ Banner/Sign Maker: Can you make signs that catch a person's eye? Try making banners and signs for schools or for people who want to get the word out about something.

Are You A Nature Lover?

$ Garden Planner: Are you an expert on plants and where they grow best? Sell your ideas about plants and flowers to neighbors whose yards could use a face-lift.

$ Fresh Foods Stand: Are you gifted with a green thumb? Maybe you should start selling delicious fruits and vegetables right out of your garden.

$ Weed Puller/Lawn Mower: Are you willing to work hard and sweat a little? Many people hate mowing their lawns and pulling weeds, so they will love the help.

$ Leaf Raker/Snow Shoveler: Do you have strong arms and a good back? People will gladly pay you for this.

We have not stated all the possibilities here, so stay open to new ideas and jobs. However, when all else fails, there is always the lemonade stand!

Advertising

Don't be afraid to be creative when you advertise: good advertising is the key to success.

Clare: To advertise my business, I distribute flyers around my neighborhood stating my name, phone number, and business. Good flyers should be creatively designed to catch a person's eye with bright colors and catchy slogans. Example: "To make sure your pet gets the BEST CARE, call Clare at 555-5555!"

Emily: When my business first started, I called friends and people I knew and asked them if they had any odd jobs I could do. When I did a good job, they told their friends, and so on. As my business grew, I began to distribute business cards and post flyers on local bulletin boards.

Other Ways To Advertise

$ Place a small ad in the classified section of the local newspaper.

$ Pass out flyers around your neighborhood.

$ Put up signs.

$ Call friends and relatives.

$ Put an ad in the school newspaper.

$ Ask parents to spread the word or pass out flyers at work.

*Safety Note: Be sure to use only your first name and phone number when advertising. And DON'T FORGET to tell your parents about your advertising.

Customers and Rates

Without your customers, you wouldn't have a business. So treat them with respect.

Clare: You should always be courteous to your customers, but don't be afraid to negotiate your rates. I base my rates on how many animals I'm sitting for and the common charge in the neighborhood.

Emily: My rates are based on the amount of manual labor and time I spend on each task. For jobs like baby-sitting, base your rates by the hour. For other jobs where you sell individual items, base your price on the cost of the materials and the time you spent making the product.

*Safety Note: If a customer makes you uncomfortable in any way, please inform your parents and avoid any further contact with that customer.

Partners

Working with partners can be a lot of fun, but you have to have rules about how to divide the profits, work, and time spent on the business. Working this way helps you to avoid many unnecessary arguments. Make sure you have a very strong friendship before working as partners, since working together may put stress on your relationship.

Things to consider before starting a partnership:

$ Is your partner loyal, trustworthy, and honest?

$ Is she someone who gets the job done?

$ Is she as interested in the business as you are?

$ Is she responsible and on time?

$ Is she patient and willing to work things out?

$ Do you think you would work well together?

Common Questions

Q: How can I fix it if my business starts failing?

A: Emily: If your business starts failing, you have to figure out what is going wrong. Try asking your customers about it. Once when I was in the process of a baby-sitting business, no one was calling me. So I asked one of my customers, and she said that I had stopped returning calls. I talked to my sister, and I found out that I received several messages which never got to me! After I returned the calls, my business increased, so discovering the problem can really help.

Q: How can I keep my customers satisfied?

A: Clare: These tips are sure to make your customers happy:
- always be on time for your job
- be courteous and polite
- always deliver the best service that you possibly can
- never say you can do something for them that isn't possible (for instance, you can't agree to water your neighbor's plants the same week you're going on vacation. Instead, politely decline the job offer and recommend someone else for the job).

If you consistently do all these things, I guarantee that your customers will trust you and be completely satisfied with you and your work.

Hopefully these ideas have helped you learn how to be a great working girl! We know that when you add your own creativity and skills, you will create a business that is sure to succeed. GOOD LUCK!!!!!

 ## Keeley's Six Business Tips

Keeley Stalnaker, age 11

❀ Dream: *to become a writer, actress, or teacher*

I have started several businesses. I now run "Keeley's Flower Mart" and I also write a magazine called "Beanie Watch." Here are six helpful tips to remember:

1) Pick a business that people really need.
2) If you aren't sure what people in your neighborhood need, conduct a survey to find out what people want. Give them some options to choose from.

3) Set the right price. If you charge too much, people won't use your service. If you charge too little, you won't make a profit.

4) Before you start, make sure you have the necessary time to spend on your business.

5) Get a notebook to keep track of sales and appointments.

6) Stay with it, don't give up, and be organized!

Room Redo:
Give Your Room A Makeover

Lauren Brooks, age 12

✕ Hobbies: *skiing, singing, acting, playing piano, playing trumpet* ♫ Hero: *K.A. Applegate* ☺ Pet peeves: *snobby people and stuffy noses* ❀ Dream: *to be a professional actress, writer, or interior decorator*

Getting Started

I chose to write about this topic because redecorating your room can be really fun! Besides, redecorating can be a big problem for girls around my age. You start getting to the point where you need to become individualized. Decorating your room to fit your personality is only one of the steps towards growing up.

Okay, here's the story. Your room looks like it did in kindergarten. You want to rip it apart. There are cluttered shelves, bare walls, pink paint and your bedspread with printed hearts. Okay, maybe it's not that bad, but it's still time for a change.

There are two things you need to do before you start redecorating. First, get your parent's permission. Next you need to get a plan! Don't charge in and start painting and ripping things apart—first decide what you want your room to look like.

Room Types

Now we're getting to the good part. You get to decide what type of room you want. Do you want a magazine-y, girlie, sophisticated, hippie, modern, or sporty type of room? If none of these categories fit you, then make up your own! Remember that the color, furniture, and decorations in your room make your room look a certain way. Where you put those items also counts. Choose a look that fits you.

Fads

One of the worst mistakes people can make when redecorating is having a fad room. A fad room is when everything in your room is based on today's fads. Unfortunately, fads go out as quickly as they come in. Who wants to paint their room a new color every month just because their color went "out" and another came "in"? The best way to avoid a fad room is to get things you know you'll like for a long time.

Models

When I say models I don't mean the models that walk down runways wearing sleek black dresses. The best way to plan your room is to make a drawing of what you're going to do—a before-and-after picture! Draw blocks on a piece of paper in the arrangement of your room, and if you're an artist you can make detailed drawings. Then label what they are and what you're going to do with them. For instance: shelf—paint white, bookcase—clean out, wall—add posters. Then when you're redecorating your room, you'll have a guide.

Accessories

Okay, your plan is in place. I suggest starting small and working up. Who knows? Maybe after a few changes of accessories and decorations, you will love your room. Then you won't have to do something huge (like painting). Some accessories that can really change your room are: pillows, lamps, curtains, rugs, a phone, a fish tank, quilts, and mirrors. Mirrors always make a room look bigger. One of my personal favorites is cheap and decorative—a bean bag chair.

Turnin' Old To New

Do you have old furniture? Did your mom buy you a lamp that you like, but you hate the lampshade? Then here's some advice for you: Before you throw stuff away, think of creative ways to improve it. This saves you money and helps the environment! Fabric can be really helpful. Just attach it onto furniture with a staple gun or hot glue gun. (Make sure you get an adult to help so you don't glue your hand to the wall.) Lampshades can be covered with fabric or trim. Remember, all your material can be bought at a second-hand store. You could also cut up old sheets or curtains that you have around the house.

Furniture

My personal favorite furniture is plastic inflatable! You don't have to worry about moving it, because it can be kicked out of your way! If you have old wooden furniture, then you can easily paint it. Desks and chairs look good when they're painted white, but you can use any color you want. Before you start painting, call a hardware store and ask for their advice. Sometimes you may need to do some sanding first. Another fun and easy thing to do with furniture is to stencil or sponge paint it. You can buy stencils or make your own. To make your own, you take a piece of posterboard and draw the design you want. Carefully cut out your design and hold it over your furniture. Paint in the stencil, being careful to stay inside the lines. Let it dry for a few seconds, and then remove the stencil. Voila! A beautiful design!

Walls

Decorating your walls is an exciting part of changing your room. The easiest way to improve your walls is by adding posters. You can buy them or make your own. If you buy them, they can be pictures of pets, places, famous people, sports, your hero, plays—anything. But whether you're artistic or not, you can make your own posters. You can do an intricate drawing, modern art (paint blobs) or 3-D collages. For a 3-D collage, take objects that you like and glue them on a piece of poster board.

Did you know that you can put up wall curtains? Go to a second-hand store and get cheap material like tablecloths, bedspreads, or curtains. Then take a staple gun and drape them around your walls. If you find a lace tablecloth, buy it! Lace looks really pretty on your walls, and if you like the color of your paint, lace will let you see through.

Paint And Wallpaper

Now for the harder stuff. For the walls you might want paint, wallpaper, or stencils. Make sure you like the patterns and colors and that they match everything in your room. If you don't want to wall paper your whole wall, you can put up a small wallpaper border on the top 6 inches (15 cm) of your wall. Stencils also look great on your walls and they can match the stencils on your furniture. Another fun alternative is to cut shapes out of sponges and dip them in paint to make sponge paintings. They look kind of like blobs of paint, but in shapes that you want.

Painting the whole wall is a hard part of redecorating. The best time to do painting is when you're moving to a new house, because there's nothing in your way. If you're not moving, you have to move everything to the middle of the room and drape it with cloth (so it doesn't get paint on it), or empty out your room. Then you have to make sure you get the right amount of paint and the right color. If you have slanted walls or ceilings you can use two different colors, one for the wall one for the ceiling. This brings out the weird shape of your room because the colors meet at the slanted corners.

Look Up!

Your walls look great, but what about the ceiling? If it seems empty, there are many things you can do to help. If you want something you can see in the daytime, use giant posters or mirrors (and get help to make sure they're secure). If you want something you can see at night, put up glow-in-the-dark, stick-on shapes.

Problems That Might Come Up

Clutter

While you are trying to redecorate, you might notice that you don't have room for anything new. It might be time for some drastic changes. You know, you might not need to save the sticker collection you had when you were five. And the puppets you made in second grade might have to go. Sometimes it's hard to get rid of things, even if you're never going to use them again. For these things, get rid of what you can and keep the rest in a keepsake box or storage. For all the stuff you want to get rid of, have a garage sale. That will help you make money to redecorate the rest of your room.

If you need more organizing help, the Container Store (1-800-786-7315) does free consultations over the phone to help organize your room!

Roommates

Do you have a sister or brother who shares your space? Well... when you redecorate it'll be either their doom or deliverance. First try to compromise with them so you can get something you both like. If they don't want to change, too bad for them. It will just have to be your side of the room that doesn't look like blah world. If you're just doing your side of the room do not put a big piece of tape down the middle of the carpet. Use a shelf, desk, or bookcase to divide the room. You might not even need to do that. It'll be obvious which side is yours, because it will totally reflect your personality.

Split-Personality Room

One of my favorite things to do when roommates don't cooperate is the split-personality room. The split-personality room is for people who are complete opposites. First you pick a place to divide the room in half. Then you each decorate your side of the room any way you want it, and if they don't match, perfect! You can even paint your side of the room one color, while they paint theirs another. Voila! A split-personality room.

Saving Money

Throughout this whole process you have to keep in mind how to save your money. If you're like me, you don't have enough money to buy everything new. And even if you did, how many parents would let their kid spend their whole savings account on a bedroom?

The best way to save is to shop smart. Go to garage sales and second-hand stores. You can have a lot of fun making things with your friends. And if you have to, I'll give you permission to buy a few things at the mall . . . as long as they're on sale.

Time To Celebrate!

When you're finished with your new and amazing room, you might want to have a sleepover celebration in it! It's a great way to show off all your hard work. If, after lots of begging, your parents still won't let you redecorate your room (boo-hoo), then helping a friend is almost as much fun! So let's get busy!

Don't Ever Give Up

Zhanna Rudnitsky, age 16

- Hobbies: *writing, reading, having fun with friends*
- Favorite writer: *Francine Pascal* Heroes: *my parents*
- Dreams: *to be an interior decorator and an author*

My Challenge

Everybody knows negative people. Sometimes negative people can convince you to give up on a dream that you have. I have learned that when someone tries to tell you that you're not smart enough to do something you want to do, you have to trust your heart and believe in yourself. Here's my story:

Moving to a new country isn't easy for a person. It wasn't easy for me. I was born in Ukraine (in Russia) and I grew up speaking only Russian. I did not know that there were other places in the world. I lived in a little town called Rokitno. It was almost like a farm town. No one was wealthy there or higher than anybody. Everyone was equal.

Coming To America

The problem was that there weren't many career options in my little town, and the economy isn't as good as it is in America. Everyone had heard of America, including me, but I never thought I would be coming to that country. But when I was eight, my parents announced that we were going to America. I was excited. Flying on the plane for the first time was amazing. I arrived in Florida and I saw nice, well-dressed adults looking at us with happy smiles. These people were our sponsors. I had never seen such wealth.

Coming to America changed my life in many ways. I learned incredible new things. On my first day in America, they fed me warm Quaker Oats with wheat bread. I thought it was so delicious. Going to the grocery store was a big adventure for me. The store was nice and neat and I had never seen so many aisles of food. I wanted to try everything. We went to a toy store and I saw all of the toys. My parents said that my eyes sparkled and that I looked so happy. Our sponsors took us to a clothing store and I got all new clothes.

Starting School

My next big challenge was starting second grade. The only English words that I knew were "hi," "bye," and the numbers one through ten. The rest I was clueless about. In second grade, the teacher tried to teach me, but I only learned how to ask basic questions and say the alphabet. The Russian language uses a completely different alphabet, and even though I tried hard to understand the new letters, I kept slipping. The teacher would always look at me with pity and shake her head. I knew she didn't like me and I felt like a failure. I didn't want to go to school because I felt like I would never learn. Every time my mom woke me up, I started crying. It hurt inside that people thought I was a failure.

After seven months my parents and I moved to Chicago. There my teacher mostly ignored me. Every day I came home clueless about what had been taught in class. The teacher expected me to learn and catch on all by myself. Luckily, two months later we decided to move to Portland. But my life there became even more challenging. I started fourth grade and I didn't even know how to read or write.

My Great Teacher

In Portland I finally got a teacher who really inspired me. Mr. Reardon showed me the states in the U.S. and asked me to learn the names and places of each one. Then he began teaching me how to write. He gave me little sentences to read and rewrite. I found it very interesting, but I kept telling him that I couldn't learn and never would. He looked me in the eye and told me, "I know you can do it. You just don't want to try." I knew he was right. I knew I could do it.

After I learned to read children's books, it became easier to read harder books. Going to the library became exciting for me. I realized that I loved reading, but writing was still hard for me. When I wrote paragraphs, they always contained mistakes. Mr. Reardon still told me not to give up. Sometimes I wanted to scream because each day there was another challenging thing for me to do. I started saying, "I can't understand because I'm Ukrainian." I thought that pretending not to understand English would excuse me from doing hard school work. It did at first, but it didn't get me anywhere. I realized I was only hurting myself.

Now I love reading, and writing is my hobby. Mr. Reardon pushed me to the limit. He knew I could do anything. Now whenever I get a hard teacher, I don't complain or give up. Instead I ask the teacher questions. I show interest and get books to help me. Most of all, I ask others for help. Hard teachers will surprise and inspire you. They are willing to help you. If you get a teacher who gives new challenges, go for those challenges. In the end you will actually feel great.

Happy Ending

It's been eight years since I came to America and it feels like I was born here. Understanding English is a breeze now. I have decided I want to help people who have just come to America and don't understand the language. I know the frustration and hopelessness they feel because I have been there, too. Of course I still have to face challenges, but I stand tall knowing I can do it. I believe you can do it, too.

How You Can Help

Each year there are many immigrants who move to the U.S. without knowing English. This makes it hard for them to get around and meet people. It also makes them feel very insecure about themselves.

If you already know English, you may know someone else who is new to this country. You could really help them out. Think about how much you would like a helping hand if you were in their situation. There are lots of ways to help. If you have classes with this person, try explaining the assignments to her. If she doesn't understand what you are talking about, then show her visually. For instance, take a pencil and point to what she has to write down on a piece of paper. Hopefully she will understand what you are trying to say, but if not, she will still appreciate your effort.

Talk to the person every time you are in class. Even if she doesn't understand you, she will eventually catch on. When I was in fourth grade, a couple of girls made a real effort to talk to me. I didn't really understand them, but they moved their hands a lot and tried to be as clear as possible and I eventually got the idea.

Hangin' Out

If you invite your friends to talk to the new person, this will help her feel more secure because she will know some people. You can have fun with her just like you would with anybody else. Ask about her country, her hobbies, or her favorite food. Be casual around her and have normal conversations as you would with any of your other friends. She will find it interesting to listen to you, and eventually she will start to understand you.

You can be reassuring to your new friend and tell her that you are there if she has any questions or needs help on homework. Assure her that people will be there when they're needed. After a while, she will progress more and find herself doing things on her own.

All this takes time. So don't expect anything soon. Most of all, just be a good friend and help the person out. This is encouraging and tells her that she can do it. My friends were by my side and tried to help me out as much as possible. It gave me a boost and I knew that there were people who cared about me.

Go For Your Dreams

My story isn't just about moving to a new country. This is all about not giving up! I believe that you can make your dreams come true and reach your goals. It all begins when you believe in yourself. Deep inside your heart you have to believe that anything can happen if you really want it to. You can learn that language, you can overcome challenges and reach goals you thought you never could.

If a situation is difficult, and you feel like you'll never win, don't turn away and think you can never do this. Because you can and you know it. Sometimes you just don't want to climb that mountain because you're afraid that you'll never make it to the top. Well, why not try it and find out?

There are times when things get difficult and you want to give up, but that won't get you anywhere. You have to ask for help. You have to make the best of it. No matter what kind of problem you have, it can be overcome with determination. Determination will take you anywhere you want to be.

Poetry Power: Having Fun With Poetry

Erica Nedelman, age 10

✂ Hobbies: *swimming, art, math* ❀ Dream: *to be an Olympic swimmer*

Lindsay Harbron, age 11

✂ Hobbies: *figure skating, arts, crafts, ballet, jazz* 🖊 Hero: *Tara Lipinski* ❀ Dreams: *to skate in the Olympics and to be an author*

Katie Rivard, age 11

✂ Hobbies: *reading, soccer, basketball, dance, art, writing* ❀ Dream: *to be the first female president of the U.S.*

Very Verse

You might think that poetry is boring and dry, but we are here to show you that there are lots of fun and crazy things you can do with poetry! When you write poetry you can have fun with your friends or you can express your feelings all by yourself.

We first learned about poetry from our fourth grade teacher, Mrs. Aprahamian. In her class we did several adventurous poetry projects and had a lot of fun. But poetry isn't just for school! There are hundreds of poetry forms, but we have chosen a few of our favorites to share with girls everywhere.

Alphabet Poems

Directions for writing an alphabet poem:

1) Choose a topic and a title. (You can write about anything!)
2) Make a list of words about your topic. Write down every crazy word you can think of.

3) Write the letters of the alphabet vertically down the left side of your paper.

4) Create a poem using the words on your list to match the letters of the alphabet.

Here's the beginning of our alphabet poem:

Michigan Is Great by Erica

Apple picking and apple cider in the fall

Biking around Mackinac Island

Crossing the bridge to the Upper Peninsula

Dairy Queen ice cream and lunch in the summer

Elmira—home of the potato burger!

You get the idea! Can you make it to "Z"?

Once you get really good at alphabet poems, there are certain tricks you can play. A famous poet who used alphabet poetry was Edgar Allan Poe. In "A Valentine" he hid his sweetheart's name in the poem! Her name is Frances, and it is hidden in the first letter of the first line, the second letter of the second line and so on.

A Valentine

by Edgar Allen Poe (1809-1849)

For her this rhyme is penned, whose luminous eyes,

B**R**ightly expressive as the twins of Loeda,

Sh**A**ll find her own sweet name, that, nestling lies

Upo**N** the page, enwrapped from every reader.

Sear**C**h narrowly the lines!—they hold a treasure

Divin**E**—a talisman—an amulet

That mu**S**t be worn at heart. Search well.

Alliteration Poems

This is probably the first kind of poem you learned about when you were young. For alliteration poems, you pick your favorite letter and repeat it over and over. These poems are also known as tongue twisters!

To write an alliteration poem:

1) Pick a fun letter
2) Think of LOTS of words that include your letter
3) Be creative and make them funny!

Using alliteration is fun and challenging. All it takes is some thought. Go ahead and try! Here is ours:

Tapping Toes by Katie
Ten teenage tap-dancers
tapped tiny toes
to a timely tune.

Cut-And-Paste Poetry

This is one of our personal favorites! It is easy to do and is really fun to try with friends. To create a cut-and-paste poem:

1) Gather magazines, scissors, glue and a piece of paper.
2) Cut out words or phrases from the magazine.
3) Arrange the phrases so they go together and glue them on a piece of paper. You can have as many lines as you wish!

Cut and Paste by Lindsay

RIGHT AT YOUR FEET.

GOOD TO EAT.

with less fat.*

for A CAT

Cinquain

The word cinquain is French for "a group of five." This poetry form was invented not long ago by an American woman! A cinquain has five lines that describe something or someone. Here is a cinquain written by the woman who invented them, Adelaide Crapsey (1878-1914).

Laurel in the Berkshires

Sea-foam

and coral! Oh, I'll

climb the great pasture rocks

and dream me mermaid in the sun's

gold flood.

Directions for creating a cinquain:

1) Choose a title.
2) The first line only has one word. This word can be the same as the title, or it can describe the title.
3) This line has two words that physically describe the title.
4) The next line has three words that express action.
5) The next line has four words that express feeling.
6) The last line has one last descriptive word.

LINDSAY

Lindsay

Delicate, Lively

Dancing, Running, Talking

Shy, Excited, Nervous, Happy

Unique

Rhyme  Poems

Rhyme is one of the most popular kinds of poetry. Poems that rhyme are fun to sing and read out loud. You can write them by following many different patterns. Did you know that all languages have rhyming words? A few English words that have no rhyme are: orange, sugar, radio, and elephant.

Directions for writing a rhyme poem:

1) Choose a topic.

2) Brainstorm for words that rhyme.

3) Write a poem using this pattern: the first and second lines rhyme together; the third and fourth lines rhyme together.

4) Make up your own rhyme patterns!

Teddy Bear by Erica
A cute little bear
with brown, furry hair
He sleeps in your bed
and lays on your head.

Free  Verse

Free verse is a type of poetry where the author creates the pattern. We like to use this form a lot because then you don't have to follow any rules—you just make up your own! Professional poets have different feelings about free verse. Robert Frost said that writing free verse is like playing tennis without a net. But many great poets such as Walt Whitman and William Carlos Williams wrote most of their poetry in free verse, and e.e. cummings didn't even use any punctuation!

The directions are simple for free verse:

1) Choose a topic.

2) Make it up! Free Verse poetry is fun to write.

Storm by Katie

As a bough swings by,

it sweeps past the stars in the night,

as it disappears from view.

Soon the air becomes colder.

The wind begins to sputter and cough,

as the peaceful night becomes more violent.

A sudden stop occurs,

calming the night's fear as a clear dawn awakens.

Limericks

Limericks are short, humorous, rhyming verses. You probably know about limericks from Mother Goose! When you write a limerick, you have 5 lines. The 1st, 2nd, and 5th lines all rhyme, and they all have 7-10 syllables. The 3rd and 4th lines each have 5-7 syllables, and they rhyme with each other.

Fay by Katie

There once was a lady named Fay,

Who studied the art of ballet.

With a turn and a jump,

she fell on her rump.

From then on she studied croquet!

Poetry Parties

Now that you know all about poetry, you can have your very own "Poetry Party!" Get a bunch of friends together to read some of your favorite poems and write poetry of your own. One fun thing to do is write a group poem together.

To write a group poem:

1) Sit in a circle with your friends.

2) Decide on your poem topic.

3) Have everyone write one line about the topic, without showing anyone else.

4) If you want, everyone can make their lines rhyme with the same word.

5) Put all the lines down on the floor, and arrange them so they go together.

6) Now you have a poem written by you and your friends!

Another fun way to write a group poem is to have everyone take a turn making up one line which they say out loud. Have one person write the lines down as people say them. Caution: if you choose a humorous topic, these poems can get really silly!

Poetry Readings

You might also be able to interest your friends in a poetry reading. Pick a place to be the "stage." Dress up like a character from the poem, or as an old-fashioned author! Then pass out hot cocoa and take turns reading your favorite poetry out loud. When we were writing this chapter, we met at a bookstore or coffee shop to drink tea and hot chocolate. We read all different kinds of poems to each other and giggled at the really silly ones. We had a lot of fun with the poems and we hope you do too! Remember that there is no such thing as "wrong" poetry. Develop your own poetic style and have a great time!

LOVING YOUR HUGGABLES

Chelsea Pyle, age 12

✄ Hobbies: *gymnastics, baseball, drawing, playing in the dirt*
🖉 Hero: *Shannon Miller* ☯ Something unusual: *I haven't worn a dress since 1992* ❀ Dreams: *to win a gold medal in gymnastics and to become an artist for Disney.*

Where's My Blankey?

Do you still have the same doll or stuffed animal that you've had since you were little? You might be feeling a little too old for them right now. Do you hide them when your friends come over because they might tease you if they know that you still have your favorite "huggable?"

Well I want to tell you that you should never give up your oldest, most faithful friends! It's okay! I still have my blankey. I've had "her" for as long as I can remember. My mom made her especially for me when I was little. My blankey is pink with little elephants, blue balloons, and a blue polka-dotted ruffle. I sleep with her cuddled around me every night, and she is the first thing I pack when I'm going to be gone overnight. Some people have teased me about her, but I plan on keeping my blankey forever, no matter what other people think or say.

Do They Tease You, Too?

I got the idea to write about huggables one day when my mom was going to wash my blankey. I always get worried that something bad will happen to my blankey when she's being washed. She might get another hole or she might come out of the dryer smaller or even a different color. My brother started teasing me for worrying so much about a "dumb, old blanket." I thought that this has probably happened to other girls, too, so I decided to write my chapter about huggables.

My blankey is very precious to me. I know that other girls have stuffed animals or teddy bears that they've had for years, too. It makes me upset when girls grow up too fast and are told that they don't need to have any "kid things" anymore. I don't want other girls to ever think that they are too old to have a huggable to comfort them.

Hey! We All Have 'Em

Most of my friends' huggables are either stuffed animals or blankeys (like mine). But a huggable isn't always something that is soft or stuffed or even something you can touch.

A huggable might be:

☺ A book that you used to read every night when you were little.

☺ A photograph that has a special spot in your heart.

☺ A symbol of who you want to be when you grow up.

☺ A song that your mom used to sing to you. Maybe you hum that familiar little tune to yourself and you feel safe wherever you are.

A huggable has a special way of sneaking into your heart. If you get a dolly when you're little, and you hold it when you're scared or sad, and hug it when you're happy or glad, you get attached to it. After sleeping with the same old teddy bear for years and years, it just seems like he has to be there at nighttime. A special stuffed animal that has been around for so long, seems almost like a part of you.

Hug And Remember

Your favorite stuffed animal, dolly, teddy bear, or blankey can help you remember special times and special people. You hold your dolly and remember that your dad got her for you on your fourth birthday. You hug your teddy bear and remember that your grandma gave him to you on the Christmas when it snowed 6 inches (15 cm). These are memories that can be taken to heart every time you hold your huggable close. Your favorite huggable can help you to remember family trips, adventures, slumber parties, or even stays in the hospital. And when you keep your gentle huggable close to you, you are keeping those special memories close to you, too.

An Unusual Friend

Sometimes, your favorite huggable can be your very best friend. A special stuffed animal is great to talk to. It will always agree with you. You can tell it how your day went and what you did in school. It can help you practice your speech for English class or your part in the school play, and make sure your homework makes sense. To your teddy bear you can explain about your problems with your friends, or the big fight you're having with your sister, and it won't ever argue with you. You might want to tell it why you're just having a bad day. If you have a secret, you can safely reveal it to your doll.

Having Fun With Your Huggable

You can also do fun things with your huggables! Here are some ideas for huggable parties:

☺ A sleep-over where all your friends bring their special huggable along with them. You and your friends can talk about the special times you've had with your huggables. You can tell about the interesting places you've visited when you've taken your huggables along.

☺ A "makeover" party, where all of you can add new ribbons and trims to your huggables.

☺ A masquerade party, or a fashion show, where you and your huggable are dressed, or decorated, to match.

☺ A tea party where you can practice your manners together—but be careful not to spill on the huggables!

Alone Time With Your Huggable

Sometimes there is nothing better than being alone. But we all
know that being alone is so much better with our huggables! Try taking
your dolly to the tree house for some nice, quiet times. You and your
huggable can have fun all by your lonesomes. For easy relaxing times,
try taking your huggable outside on a nice, sunny day to lie in the
hammock with you, to watch the flowers grow and the clouds go by.

A Huggable Makeover

You might want to decorate your huggable to keep it looking spiffy
and new. Maybe your teddy bear needs some new, brown buttons on his
vest. Does your dolly need a new, shiny bow in her hair? Maybe your
favorite book needs a new cover protector. Or what about making an
old, framed photograph a little more sparkly? Decorating huggables with
sequins, buttons, colorful thread or ribbons, or puff paints can make
your quiet friend look even more beautiful on the outside than it
already is. But your huggable will always be beautiful to you on the
inside, and you don't have to do anything to beautify it there, where it
matters the most.

Patch Work

If your gentle friends are a little sad and worn, a little tired and
torn, or even a little shabby and forlorn, it just means that they are
well-loved. Don't feel like your favorite old teddy bear is lacking in
charm if he is sort of flat and his hair is kind of matted. If your dolly's
hair gets kind of wild, it just means she's been held a lot. But if your
stuffed animal gets a hole in its ear, be sure to give it some tender loving care and sew it back up.

My blankey had a little problem a few years ago. She had many,
many tiny little holes (because I do love her so very, very much) and I
was so afraid she was going to fall apart. So my mom made a special

blanket for her to go inside so she would not get any more little holes. She's still the same lovable blankey on the inside, where it counts. When you love your favorite huggable, you just love it, no matter what shape it's in, or what it looks like after many years. Don't be ashamed of your old bear or your shaggy stuffed animals. All that matters is the love they give you when you need it the most!

Standing Up For Your Huggable

Do you get embarrassed when other people make fun of you and your blankey? Do they tell you you're too old, too big, too cool, or too tough to still keep your favorite doll around? Some people might make fun of you for having a huggable. Try not to let them bother you. You don't have to listen to them—just ignore them. You could tell them that you love your huggable and you don't care if they make fun of you. You could also say that your huggable has been your friend for a long time and it has never been mean to you, unlike some people....

The person making fun of you probably had a huggable of their own when they were younger. Sometimes parents feel that it's time for us to grow up, and they throw out our huggables! If you can believe it, they might even burn someone's blankey!! So the person who is teasing you might not have their huggable any more, due to this sort of cruel torture. They are probably teasing you because they miss their huggable, and they are just jealous.

Don't let other people make you think that you shouldn't have a huggable. Don't be ashamed of being attached to your favorite things. You don't ever have to give them up! Remember that you can have a huggable, no matter what age you are. Someone might tease you about still having your favorite dolly that has been around for years and years. Someone might make fun of you, telling you you're too old to love your teddy bear. Don't believe them for one minute. I've had the best times with my blankey, from cuddling with my dad while we watched TV, to going to slumber parties with my friends. I'm not ashamed to keep my blankey forever. How about you??

What To Do When Your Best Friend Ditches You

Rachel Holihan, age 14

✂ Hobbies: *softball, basketball, reading, writing, singing, acting* ☹ Pet peeves: *hypocrites and mean people*
❀ Dream: *to be a freelance writer or a columnist for* The Chicago Tribune

Has this happened to you? You lose all your close friends. You don't know why. You know you didn't do anything that could make them hate you this much. So why are they doing this? It is hard to go up and ask them because you feel intimidated. Anyway, they never look back to see how much damage they've done. See! You're not the only one. I know how you feel. You don't have to feel alone because it has happened to tons of girls, including myself.

Before The Storm

Seventh grade was going great. I kept all my friends from elementary school and had even added some new ones. We had our "group" and we did everything together. I was especially close to my best friend, Amber.* I never did anything without her. Well, not until she started to do things without me. Amber and two other friends in our group, Lillie and Meredith, started doing everything together. That was okay with me, but then they began to purposely exclude me. They would talk about what they were going to do together in front of me, but they never invited me.

---

*All names have been changed to protect the innocent and not-so-innocent.

Rough Weather

I went along with this for a couple of weeks. Then one day Meredith just stopped talking to me completely. My bad day got even worse when I was talking with another friend about it and she said, "They don't like you. They don't want to be friends with you anymore." Could she have been any more blunt? I mean, she could have laid it on me softly—I felt like she had thrown a ton of bricks on my soul. I felt so alone that I was practically in tears. I wanted it to be a bad dream, but it wasn't. I felt like I didn't matter to anybody.

All Alone

Soon my other friends were ignoring me, too. I was pretty much all alone except for a few casual friends. It was horrible. There were nights when I cried and felt sorry for myself, and other times when I wrote in my journal and tried to be happy. But either way, it seemed like all that really mattered to me was gone. I would have rather been hurt physically than go through so much emotional pain. I should have talked about the pain to someone, but instead I just let myself be miserable, pretending that I had millions of friends even though I didn't.

Reasons Why

I never found out why my "friends" decided to drop me. But I wondered about it every day. Sometimes I put the blame on myself and wondered if it was because I wasn't thin enough, pretty enough, popular enough, or maybe because I wanted to be nice to everyone, not just the popular kids.

Blaming myself for their actions was wrong, though. If this happens to you, never blame yourself! Chances are it isn't your fault. Your friends might not even know why they aren't friends with you anymore. If any of their reasons have to do with looks, popularity, guys, or any other stupid reason, then they don't deserve to have you as a friend.

Recovering

Finally I began making other friends. School let out for the summer and things were better because there wasn't anyone around to remind me of what had happened. I went on vacation with my older cousin Clare and she really helped me understand that I wasn't alone in this. It had happened to her, too—even in college. You aren't alone either. Looking back, I wish I had asked for help and talked about it sooner, because it helped so much when I did.

Why Are Girls So Mean?

I never knew how mean girls could be until my friendship with Amber, Meredith, and Lillie ended. Even after our friendship had stopped they still said mean things to me. One day when we were doing track and field, Amber came up to me and said, "Did you even get over the hurdles?" I said, "Yes," and she retorted "That's right, you fell and looked really stupid. You are really bad at the hurdles." I wanted to smack her in the face, but I didn't. During the summer, my mother was having a party and she invited Meredith's mother over. Unfortunately, she brought Meredith with her. The whole time Meredith was at my house, she made fun of me behind my back.

Sometimes I wish we would fight like boys do. One of my guy friends said to me, "Why don't girls just fight like guys? In 10 minutes it would be over and you wouldn't have lost any friends."

I answered, "Girls fight with words. We are so catty and harsh to each other. We are cruel. And it is hard to forgive somebody who is cruel."

The Power of Words

This reminds me of the saying, "Sticks and stones may break your bones, but words can never hurt you." That has to be one of the biggest lies I've ever heard. Words do hurt. They leave permanent marks on people that cannot be erased. When you break a bone it hurts, but the pain goes away and you can forget about it. The pain of words you do not forget. You remember that kind of pain forever.

We have to be careful about what we say. The words that come out of our mouths can easily cause permanent emotional damage. There are many times that we do not realize we are being mean. If you do notice, apologize. If someone is being mean to you, stand up for yourself. If you don't, they will just keep bugging you.

Standing Up For Yourself

Brittany Bennett, age 11

Hero: *Tara Lipinski* ❀ Dream: *to become a world-famous writer*

A Bossy Bully

Standing up for yourself is a hard thing to do, especially if you have never had to before. Last year one of my friends suddenly changed when we were out of school for the summer. She did her best to avoid me, and if another girl tried to talk to me, she would kick them so they would stop talking. After school I would go to my mom and tell her how awful my day was, and sometimes I would cry. When the girl was mean to me, I didn't know what to say. I would cry or look really upset.

One day my mom explained that if I wanted to get this girl to stop, I had to stand up to her. I was like, "Oh, easy for you to say. You don't have to put up with her!" But I finally found the courage. The next time she was mean to me, I completely ignored her, and looked like I couldn't care less. Surprisingly, she started being much nicer to me! I realized that when I didn't react, she got bored really fast. I know it is hard to take a stand, but it really works.

Take A Stand

If you are having trouble like this, it's not like you have to go through it alone. You can talk to parents, relatives, other friends, or guidance counselors. There are many people to talk to, but they can't solve your problems for you. You have to be the one to take action! Never, ever, let anyone push you around.

Here's how:

1) Try to completely ignore them. Act like you don't see them, hear them—nothing! Eventually they should get bored.

2) Try the rational approach. In your strongest voice, say "Why are you doing this?" It will probably shock them.

3) Make them feel guilty. When you are alone with them say "You know, that hurts my feelings. How would you like it?"

4) Steal their thunder. When they tease you, agree with them and laugh about it. What can they say?

5) If you really get desperate, or they do something that is really mean, then tell an adult about it.

Standing up for yourself is big. I mean BIG! It helps you:

☺ Tell people how you feel.

☺ Stop people from hurting you or others.

☺ Stay happy so you won't dread each day.

More Reasons Why They're Mean

Girls tend to pick on peers who have something they don't have. They are mean to girls who are smart, confident, pretty, assertive— anyone who is something they are not. They are also cruel to anyone who is the least bit different. Maybe it's because someone has a different religion, or because they're from another country, or maybe it's even because they think someone is too tall, too short, too skinny, too large, or not popular enough. They also tend to focus their criticism on a girl who is basically happy with herself and the world. In other words, they pick on girls they're jealous of.

One reason that girls are mean is that they don't feel happy with themselves, so they put down someone else in order to feel like they are okay. Attacking someone else makes them feel they are better than other people. This isn't a good excuse! Girls shouldn't be doing this to each other. Once you have felt the pain of cruel words, you know what I am talking about.

Sisterhood

One thing I have learned from all this is that girls are too harsh to each other. We need to stop cutting each other down, and start helping each other out more. Girls everywhere share the bond of sisterhood—I mean we all go through the same things, and we should take care of each other. If we united as girls and helped each other out, imagine how strong we could be!

Put A Little Love In Your Heart

I know you might have heard this phrase over and over: "Treat others as you would like to be treated." Sometimes it's hard to know how to act around others. Listen to yourself talk. If somebody was saying the same thing to you, would it hurt your feelings? If it would, then chances are you are hurting their feelings.

Too many people get picked on. Too many people go home and cry after school because classmates tease them and make them miserable. I used to be one of the criers. Make people's lives happier. If you try to be nice to everyone, then chances are they will be nice to you, too. I mean, what's it going to hurt? I've never heard of anything drastically bad happening because someone was nice.

How Do I Get Over It?

Getting over friends' cruelty can be very hard and takes a lot of time. It has been a year since I was friends with Amber, Lillie, and Meredith, and I'm just getting over the loss of my friends. The worst time is the period before you make new friends. Here are some tips to help you through that time:

- Talk to someone. I waited too long to do that. You could talk with a counselor, a parent, older siblings, a friend, or another adult you trust. I am going to therapy now and it has helped me tremendously. Just getting your feelings out makes you feel much better.
- Punch a pillow. Imagine that the pillow is the person that hurt you and take it out on the pillow.
- Journal writing helps also. You can put all your feelings down on the paper and no one will ever read it.
- Write a letter to your friend telling her how you feel. Make sure it's not mean, just express your pain.

Making New Friends

After going through something like this, you will want to find true friends. Different people have different traits, but true friends have many of the same qualities. True friends: • love you unconditionally • are honest and trustworthy • will forgive you for mistakes • are kind and caring • stick by you in good times and bad • understand you and if they don't, they try • don't give up on you.

It may take a long time to find friends like this. It took me almost a year to find them, but now I understand how great true friends are.

True Friends Forever

Before you can find your true friends, you need to know what kind of person you are. Make some lists about what your ambitions are, what you want to be like, the good qualities a friend should have, what you like to do, and what your values are. After you look at your lists, you'll have a better understanding of who you are. This will help you to make good choices about friends. Remember that true friends aren't easy to find, but they are definitely worth waiting for.

I met each of my true friends in a different way. I met one at church, one at an after-school activity, and one when she was ditched by her friends, too. There are many other ways to make friends:

☺ Get involved in sports or other activities that interest you.

☺ Talk to people in your classes you don't know very well, or who are outside of your "group." You'll be surprised by how nice a lot of kids are.

☺ Look for other kids who seem to be alone, too. They may be having the same problems with friends that you are. They will be thrilled to have a buddy.

Forgiving Them

Forgiving. Oh, boy. I think this is the hardest part. Before you forgive you are in so much pain. But afterwards—it's amazing! You feel totally free. Forgiving is really hard, though, and it can take a lot of time. Before I forgave Amber, I used to notice every little thing she did and I thought it was all against me. I also got extremely jealous of her. But now I don't care about what she does or who she does it with.

I am happier now than I've ever remembered being. That's because I've let go. That's what you have to do. It is time to move on to better times ahead. Forgiving takes time, but it sets you free from the pain.

What I Learned

Looking back, I am kind of glad this happened. I am a better person now. When I was friends with Amber, I wasn't exactly the nicest person in the world. I could be mean and judgmental. I'm not like that now. I've learned how important it is to be nice to everybody, even the people I don't really understand. I like my friends better now, too. I am so much at ease when I talk to them—it's like I belong with them.

You've probably learned something from your own experiences, too. Whether it's about being nice, or about making new friends, apply what you've learned to your everyday life. It will make the world a better place, and then what happened will be worth it.

Friendship Triangles

Ashley Baker, age 11

❀ Dream: *to win a gold medal at the Olympics in softball*

Three Is A Crowd

Friendship triangles can be really hard. I learned how hard they can be when I became best friends with a girl named Victoria in second grade. We did everything together for two years, but all that changed in fourth grade when a girl named Candace started hanging around with Victoria and me. Suddenly, Victoria didn't pay as much attention to me as before. We always chatted together during lunch, but Candace ate lunch really fast so she could play before the bell rang. Soon Victoria started copying Candace and I found myself eating alone.

Going Solo

After school and on the weekends, Victoria and Candace started spending time together and they didn't include me. I tried to be Candace's friend but she never had much to say to me. After several tries at getting to know her, I finally just gave up. Victoria paid less and less attention to me, and we began to argue over dumb stuff. We totally drifted apart and I was really lonely.

Moving On

Finally I found some of my old friends that I had known since kindergarten. I had things in common with them and enjoyed hanging out with them. At lunch time we all ate slowly and talked. After I hung out with these girls for a couple of weeks, they started inviting me over to their houses and we started going to the movies and the mall.

I still talk with Victoria sometimes. In my heart I still think of her as a good friend. Friendship triangles are really tough. If you're in one, remember: • stay true to yourself • meet new friends or get re-acquainted with old friends • don't be cruel to your former friends.

 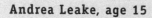

Six Steps to Recovery

Andrea Leake, age 15

❀ Dream: *to show my paintings in an art gallery*

Through The Grape Vine

In eighth grade, I became best friends with a girl. Over the summer I tried to get in touch with her, but she never seemed to be home. The whole summer went that way. Right before school began again, I started to hear from mutual friends the horrible things she was saying about me. All of the complaints she had about me were petty, not things one would say about their best friend. I felt terrible—betrayed. I'd poured out my soul to this person and there she was, gossiping about me. At school, we avoided each other and never spoke. I was really sad about it for a long time, but slowly I was able to let go.

Six Steps to Save You

Here are six steps that really helped me:

1) True friends treat each other with consideration and thoughtfulness. If you were really friends, they wouldn't be treating you this way.

2) If the person doesn't like or accept you the way you are, they aren't the type of friend you want anyway.

3) Don't let just one friend mean the world to you. Remember that there are many people who care about you, so spend more time with them instead.

4) Do activities that you love. Don't stop doing the things that make you happy, and soon you will feel better.

5) When your friends and family see that you are hurt, their first reaction is going to be to help you feel better. Let them cheer you up.

6) Remember that your life will go on and eventually it won't hurt so much anymore. No matter what it feels like now, time will heal the pain.

Are You Left-Brained Or Right-Brained?

Kira Houston, age 15

✃ Hobbies: *writing, reading, skiing* ☺ Pet peeve: *closed-minded, inflexible people* 🕮 Hero: *my mother* ❀ Dream: *to write for television shows*

Use Your Brain

Did you ever wonder why your best friend understands math so well while you just can't seem to get it? Or why your little cousin has the natural ability to draw so well? I wondered about this myself until I found out about the different sides and functions of the brain. This helped me to understand that everyone's brain works a little differently!

The brain has two sides, called the right hemisphere and the left hemisphere. Each of the two sides brings out different abilities in you. Take this quiz to find out if you're right-brained or left-brained. This quiz will teach you about yourself and help you understand what you're good at.

Quiz Time!

Directions: To see which side of the brain you use more, **photocopy the following quiz**, then complete Part 1 and Part 2. On your photocopy, circle the statements in Part 1 and Part 2 that best apply to you. Be very honest with yourself.

Part 1

☆ I almost never procrastinate.

☆ When I am taking a test in school, I always read through the entire test before beginning.

☆ I keep a daily journal.

☆ When I have a problem, it is usually easy for me to analyze it and find a solution.

☆ My room is almost always spotlessly clean.

☆ When I've lost something, I mentally trace my steps back to where I last saw it.

☆ I couldn't survive one day without wearing a watch.

☆ I do well in math class.

☆ I strongly believe there is a right and wrong to every decision.

☆ I have considered being a doctor or an accountant someday.

TOTAL: _____

Part 2

☆ I am often late getting places.

☆ I enjoy drawing and/or painting.

☆ I think I have Extrasensory Perception (ESP).

☆ I use my hands a lot when I'm talking.

☆ When I am confused, I usually trust my own judgment.

☆ I almost never read directions before doing something.

☆ It seems to me that time flies when you are having fun.

☆ I have considered being an author, a politician, or a dancer when I grow up.

☆ I can tell if someone's lying by looking into their eyes.

☆ I believe that there are two sides to every story.

TOTAL: _____

What's The Score?

Add up the circled answers in both parts. If Part 1 has more, you rely more on your left brain. If Part 2 has more, you rely more on your right brain. If your totals are the same or vary by only one or two points, you tend to use both sides of your brain equally.

Use Your Thumbs

Another way to tell if you are right-brained or left-brained is to clasp your hands together (entwining your fingers). Whichever thumb is underneath the other one is the side of the brain that you use most.

Left-Brainers Are...

...logical and analytical. You probably do well in math, science, or history. You always follow a schedule and love routines. You probably eat, sleep, and do your homework at the same times every day. You thoroughly plan everything before doing it. Your friends are always asking you for advice because they can rely on you to give them practical and sensible advice without letting feelings interfere too much.

Right-Brainers Are...

...creative and imaginative. You might have a natural flair for art or music. You believe that everyone should just go with the flow. You may not like schedules or routines. Your friends often ask you for advice because your emotional suggestions always make someone in need feel better. Basically, to you there is not just one right way of doing things and there are no wrong answers.

What If I'm Both?

If your results show that you use both sides of your brain equally, don't panic! You are perfectly normal. It doesn't mean that something is wrong with you, it just means that you are a very well-rounded person. Most of us use both sides of our brains to some degree. For instance, you may play an instrument in the band and enjoy math. There are some subjects which use both brain sides equally, like English and architecture.

For those who definitely rely on one side or the other, it can be a great experience to step out of your brain's "comfort zone" and challenge yourself!

How Right-Brainers Can "Think Left"

Follow the Yellow Brick Road

At the beginning of the week, write out a schedule to follow. Write a complete itinerary of your day including times you wake up, eat, sleep, and do your homework. Try your very best to abide by it for one week. And remember, just because you are following a routine doesn't mean that it has to be strict and orderly (e.g. a brisk walk after breakfast). Be creative. If you want to take a few hours each day to "chill out"—go for it. As long as it's on your schedule, it's legal!

Have Some Class

Whether it is over the summer or during the school year, surrender to one of those classes that you thought you'd never be able to float your boat through. You'll never know what the other side of your brain is up to unless you explore it. This doesn't mean that you have to turn into the science maniac who sits next to you in art class and recites the Laws of Physics in alphabetical order during his free time. There are many different levels to learn on. And if you do fall into the mean cracks and crevices of some analytical traps, you'll always have your right brain to bail you out.

Clean Your Room

That's right. And I mean really clean it. Your left brain helps you keep things neat and orderly. Go a little further than your average Saturday morning tidy-up. Venture through your closet or start identifying all of those weird objects under your bed. Cleaning isn't just about getting rid of dirt; it's about separating your sneakers from your dress shoes. It's about lining up your nail polish collection on your dresser from lightest color to darkest color. It's about giving your room a personality. You know, a clean one.

How Left-Brainers Can "Think Right"

Tune Out

When you get home from a mind-boggling day at school, instead of starting your homework right away, chill out. Try taking a nature walk. Close your eyes and drink in the sunshine and the sounds. Try to get yourself into a mellow mood while you slide into total relaxation. While doing this, if you feel like you are wasting valuable time, don't worry; your left side of the brain won't let you slip too far! It's always on duty, even when you tune it out.

Try It On!

Stuck inside on a rainy day? Explore your drawers and closets and create new, exhilarating outfits out of your basics. Start by loading your stereo with your favorite CD's and letting it run on a SHUFFLE cruise control. Then mix and match all of your tops, bottoms, and accessories. You will be surprised at how much fun this is, and how easy it is to mesh your clothes together. When you use your imagination, you can create anything. From a lion, to a witch, to a wardrobe!

Hakuna Matata

It means no worries. Go for a certain period of time and experiment with taking things more lightly. Take a break from analyzing everything to the shivering bone. Take a walk on cloud nine, literally! For example, instead of planning a stroll in a particular direction, let your intuition guide you. Follow your instincts and let your emotions make the decisions. If you stumble across a problem that you are confused about, don't stress over causes and effects. Why not let your heart decide?

Which Side Of The Brain Is Better?

Is one side of the brain actually better than the other? This frequently asked question can be answered in several different ways. Until fairly recently, it seemed that the right side of the brain "got no respect." Have you noticed that left brain skills are more valued in our society? The left side of the brain comes in handy with schoolwork like essay writing, science, and math. Left brains can be very logical, but both left and right brains can do well in school. People are smart in many different ways. Some people may be a valedictorian, while others may make every basketball shot they take in their life, while others can find their way out of the middle of the woods without a map or a compass to guide them.

Lately, more and more recognition is being given to the creative right brains of the world. Our society is noticing what a gift creativity and intuitiveness is, and that those skills need to be brought out in a human being just as much as they need the logic to perform the 3 Rs. Scientists have found "right-brained" problems that the logical left brain can't figure out.

Glad To Have A Brain

Both sides of the brain can be useful when on your side. Some of us are logical and organized about everything. Others let their minds wander and let the flow wash them against the banks of life. Whichever side you use most, be proud to lead it. Not everyone has your qualities and no one in this world is quite like you. Each side of the brain can go as far as you want it to and both sides will be appreciated in their own ways. Right-brained or left-brained, we're glad to have one. Is one side really better than the other? Time will tell.

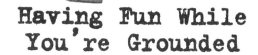

Having Fun While You're Grounded

Rebecca Kane, age 14 (left)

✄ Hobbies: *basketball, soccer, reading, shopping*

✎ Favorite class: *math* ❀ Dream: *to be an actress*

Zoe Orcutt, age 14 (right)

✄ Hobbies: *clarinet, soccer, basketball, reading, hanging out with friends, interior decorating* ☹ Pet peeve: *people who think they're perfect* ❀ Dream: *to be happy and successful*

It Happens To Everyone

We chose this topic because every girl gets grounded sometime. Just because you get grounded doesn't mean you have to sit home all day after school, bored out of your mind. We know you probably can't change your parents' decision, but we know that even when you're grounded, there are other ways to have fun!

Creative Communication

When you're grounded, your parents will most likely ground you from using the telephone, seeing friends, and leaving the house. Every girl knows that one of the hardest things about being grounded is not being able to talk with your friends, but we're here to tell you that the phone is not the only way to communicate! After you try our fun chatting ideas, you might want to stick with them even when you are free again.

Good Old Postal Service

If you are grounded for a long time, letters are a good way to communicate. Unlike phone calls, letters that you write to your friends become great memories to hold on to. You can also have a lot of fun making them look beautiful! When you write to your friends, make sure that you ask plenty of questions so they will have a good reason to write you back.

Lovely Letters

To make your letters truly lovely, you can try the following:
- Spray them with perfume.
- Use colorful markers and pencils to make them bold.
- Put crazy stickers on them.
- Include a surprise! Put tiny sparkles or confetti in the envelope so when it is opened they fly out with the letter.
- Draw fun and entertaining pictures.
- Make collages with glue and pictures from magazines.

Excellent E-mail

If you are lucky enough to have Internet access, then all your communication problems are solved! The great thing about e-mail is that it gets to your friend as fast as a phone call, and you can send the same message to two, five, or even 100 people at the same time. E-mail is great, because it's fast, quiet, and quick. The person you're writing to will most likely write you back the same day!

E-mail Decorations

Even though you can't use glitter when you e-mail, there are still some exciting ways to liven up your mail.
- Type in a colored font.
- Make cool background colors.
- Use crazy fonts.
- Some computers have clip art that you can attach with your e-mail.

Chat Rooms

When you're on-line, you can go into private chat rooms with a bunch of your friends. If you want to let your friends know that you will be in a chat room, catch them at school and say something like, "Chat room 45 at 4:15."

Secret  Codes

Whether you are writing a letter or e-mail, secret codes are really fun to use. They are especially useful if the friend you're writing to has a nosy family. Here are two codes to try out, but you can also make up more.

Shopping List Code

With this code you pretend that you're writing a shopping list. Only your friend will know differently. To address this letter so they know it's to them, you can write "Sarah's Shopping List" at the top. Down below you write your list, but the first letter of each item spells your secret message. For example, Sarah's Shopping List: • Ice • Lamps • Oranges • Violins • Eggplant • Yogurt • Ovaltine • Umbrellas. If you crack the code by taking the first letter of each item, you will find the secret message is "I LOVE YOU."

Know Your Numbers Code

In the number code, letters get replaced by numbers. If you use this code you must give them the key to crack the code at school. Example of Key: T=1, O=2, P=3, S=4, E=5, C=6, R=7. Example of Written Code: 123 456751. When your friend cracks this code she will find a TOP SECRET message. She will know that she is supposed to meet you at your secret place after school.

Entertaining Yourself

When you are done communicating with your friends, you may still need some fun activities to pass the time. Here are some great suggestions for having fun on your own.

Redecorate Your Bedroom

Zoe: When I get grounded I go up to my room and think about how I can change it. I like to cut pictures out of magazines and make collages on my wall. I also like to change my furniture around. You could hang pictures of your friends around your room, and hang things from your ceiling like curled ribbons, streamers or tie-died cloth. Read the "Room Redo" chapter in this book for more ideas.

Procrastinated Projects

Rebecca: When I am home alone I like to get caught up on all the things that I have been putting off. I usually have to catch up on cleaning my room or doing chores. You can also catch up on any missing homework. When I have homework to do that I have been putting off, I just buckle down and do it. If you can get those things done when you're grounded, then when you're un-grounded you won't have to worry about it, and you can do stuff you really enjoy.

Alone Time

Spending time alone is sometimes good so you can just calm down and relax. Read a good book, write stories, or start a journal. Or have a day of beauty! Do your nails, give yourself a facial, put on a mud mask, try out new crazy hair styles, and just have fun!!!!

Silly Siblings

You might not think that your siblings are very exciting, but sometimes they are a lot of fun. Who knows, you might actually get to know each other and become friends. With your brothers or sisters you could get some exercise. Go out for a game of basketball, soccer, volleyball, or just take a nice walk. You could also make cookies, muffins, or any other treats you both find delicious.

How To Avoid Grounding Next Time

Zoe: You get grounded for doing something that you know you shouldn't, so remember to think before do the same thing again. All grown-ups say you must think before you do something, but it's hard sometimes, especially when your friends are involved. Believe me, I know this from first-hand experience, but you still must try.

Rebecca: Whenever you get grounded you should try to think about what you did and learn from your mistakes so you don't do the same thing over again. But when you are grounded, remember our advice! It doesn't have to be the end of the world, and you actually might have a little fun.

Seeing Isn't Always Believing

Aimee Paulson, age 15

✂ Hobbies: *hockey, softball, track, piano* ☺ Pet peeve: *people who tease and make fun of others and judge people by appearance only* ❀ Dream: *to become a scientist and to find a cure for cancer*

The topic I chose to write about is self-image—learning to accept yourself. I chose this topic because self-image is a big issue for me, many of my friends, and girls in general. If girls can't accept themselves for who they are, they will run into problems as they get older.

The Media's Effect

Many things affect the way we think and feel about ourselves, and sometimes we don't even realize it. Lots of girls have self-esteem issues, and most of the time these issues can be traced back to sources in our society. For example, television, magazines, store ads, and billboards can affect the way we think and feel about ourselves. Why? Because we see the way they portray women and life, and we feel like that is supposed to be normal.

The media bombardment starts at a very young age. When we were children, boys played war with G.I. Joes and girls played house with Barbie dolls. Young children are sent the message that boys are supposed to be tough and strong, while girls are supposed to be thin and beautiful. When was the last time you played with an overweight Barbie doll? Barbies don't look like people in real life—they are all the same size, height, shape, and color. This sends girls the message that we have to try and look like models.

Everywhere you go, there are advertisements. When you're driving to the mall, you pass by billboards. At stores you see posters of models. Turn on the TV and there are commercials. All the people used for advertisements have something in common: they're all beautiful. Also, they are mostly women because women tend to shop more than men. The media advertises women using products so they will want to buy them.

Many teenage girls idolize female models and actresses because of their beauty. On television shows and in teen magazines, thin and beautiful girls are endlessly popular. This sends girls the message that being popular is extremely important and that to be well-liked you have to be thin and gorgeous.

This message is devastating to girls, and sometimes girls are willing to do anything to look like models and actresses. This often leads to dangerous eating disorders such as anorexia and bulimia. Here are two real-life stories of girls who overcame these disorders.

 ## My Struggle With Anorexia

Katie Raney, age 16
❀ Dream: *to be a policewoman*

I've always been told I was skinny. I liked thinking of myself as a skinny person. Then one day I thought, "What if I get fat?" I started worrying more and more about my weight and the panic to stay thin grew and grew. It started with just skipping a meal now and then and progressed to not eating for days at a time. My life had turned all around. Instead of worrying about normal teenage things, my thoughts revolved around food.

Slowly I got thinner and thinner until people started telling me all the time that I was really skinny. Eventually I realized that they didn't mean it as a compliment. My mom had many serious talks with me and helped me to realize how much I was hurting myself. I mean, I really could have died before I was 15!

When I had finally recovered from that harmful disease, I was happy with myself for the first time in almost a year. I know now that being healthy is 100% better than being too thin. Now I realize that true beauty is confidence in yourself and acceptance of who you are.

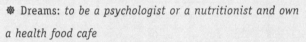

My Struggle With Bulimia

Crystal Wilkes, age 16

❀ Dreams: *to be a psychologist or a nutritionist and own a health food cafe*

I struggled with bulimia for one year, and I overcame it. I used bulimia as a way to deal with the stress in my life. When I got stressed I would overeat (bingeing), then make myself throw up (purging). This cycle ruins your teeth, disrupts your stomach's natural ability to digest food, and can eventually lead to death.

The truth is, every person needs a way to deal with stress. Some people just choose to deal with the stress better than others. Many girls play sports or have a job. My crutch used to be bulimia. Now I deal with stress by playing volleyball and working out several times a week. Doesn't that sound like a better alternative than bingeing and purging?

After struggling with bulimia, I finally began to realize that throwing up doesn't take away pain or stress, it just postpones it for later.

Warning Signs Of Eating Disorders

☞ Even though people tell you that you are too thin, you still see yourself as fat.

☞ Food and getting fat is all you think about.

☞ You constantly compare how much you eat with others, and you feel guilty if you eat more than they do.

Tips for Loving Life Again

🔥 Move your body instead of just looking at it! Play a sport, where you will be focusing on the sport and releasing energy.

🔥 Establish long-term goals for yourself like overcoming shyness, talking more with your parents, or developing a talent.

🔥 Be a rebel and stop hating your body! If you are frustrated by the fact that everywhere you look, girls and women are portrayed as wispy waifs, realize that this is nothing more than media manipulation. Love your body!

If You Want To Seek Help

☎ The National Eating Disorder Organization gives resources and information. (918-481-4044 or www.laureate.com)

☎ The National Association of Anorexia, Bulimia, and Associated Disorders is a national help and advice hotline. (847-831-3438)

☎ *The Eating Disorders Resource Catalog* contains many helpful resources and can be ordered free by calling 1-800-756-7533 or at www.bulimia.com.

☎ *Food Fight* by Janet Bode is a powerful book about eating disorders written especially for teens and preteens.

☎ *Hunger Pains* by Dr. Mary Pipher is for high school girls.

Inner Beauty VS. Outer Beauty

Beauty is everywhere, but some types of beauty are easier to spot than others. Outer beauty is the easiest to see because it is physical. A person might have really beautiful facial features or a nice smile. Inner beauty is completely different. You don't need eyes to see inner beauty. You feel it with your heart. Inner beauty comes from within and shows in girls who are kind, intelligent, funny, brave, thoughtful, or confident.

The people who are the most beautiful on the outside are not necessarily the most beautiful on the inside. Inner beauty is the only true beauty because while outer beauty deteriorates with age, your beautiful inner soul stays with you for as long as you live.

How Peers Mold Us

For girls, the opinions of peers are really important. In adolescence, most girls are insecure about their bodies and their emotions. Many girls who were adventurous in elementary school become afraid to stand out and say, "Here I am world!" in junior high and high school.

Girl Talk

Girls are already hard enough on themselves. It doesn't help when peers attack each other to protect their own insecurities. Girl talk and gossip can seem harmless, but it can do a lot of damage to a girl's self-esteem. Some girls feel better about themselves when they make others look worse. This is a very negative way to boost your self-esteem, and it can really hurt other people! Plus, girls who make fun of others are usually just jealous or insecure. If they felt good about who they are, they wouldn't have to pick on other girls. It is especially important never to make rude comments about people's weight. Cruel comments can lead to depression, eating disorders, and worse.

Boy Talk

When it comes to criticizing girls, boys are often guilty too. Some guys joke about a girl's body size or shape. They are probably just looking for a way to tease you, or to entertain their friends at your expense, but it is no excuse for their rude and hurtful behavior. Kids don't realize how much they affect each other. Some don't like to admit that they're affected by their friends and others their age, but we all are. Adolescence is a time of constant striving for acceptance, and even little things said by peers affect the way girls feel about themselves.

Striving For Perfection

The first and most important thing you need to know about perfection is: it's a lie! No one is perfect. Perfection doesn't exist in real life. Television shows and movies may portray some people's lives as perfect, but it is artificial. It is hard to accept that no one is perfect, but all you can do is your personal best, so be proud of it. Mistakes are how we learn—we all make them. Many important discoveries were made by mistake! The world is full of mistakes that are beneficial. Can you imagine how boring the world would be if everyone did everything perfectly?

Be Yourself

If you are tired of trying to be like someone you are not, then stop trying. Be yourself! This is the most powerful suggestion you could ever take. Don't let fear keep you from expressing your opinions just because others might not agree. When we disagree, we learn from each other. Everyone is different and unlike any other person. It is important to keep in touch with your inner voice. Being yourself sometimes means agreeing with others, and sometimes it means disagreeing. Being true to yourself is the important part, regardless of what everyone else does.

Create Confidence

If you are looking for ways to feel better about yourself, I have some ideas for you!

- **Pursue your passion!** What you love is a big part of who you are. When you do the things you love you will build your self-confidence.

- **Volunteer!** Participating in community service or volunteer work can make you feel good about yourself, and you will be helping others at the same time. It's a great opportunity to apply yourself and to bring joy to others.

- **Develop a new talent!** Try something you have never tried before. Go out on a limb and learn to make stained glass— or anything else you might be interested in!

- **Combat the media** with your own version of beautiful. When you see an advertisement, remember our section about inner beauty. Think about how you are beautiful inside and out!

- **Spend time getting to know you.** Spend some one-on-one time with the girl you know best—you! Write in a journal, think about who you are, and what you value. Discover you!

 ## Is Seeing Really Believing?

Tiffany Pan, age 10

❀ Dream: *to be a surgeon*

Everybody knows the saying "Seeing is believing." However, if you always believed your eyes, you would think that the sun revolves around the earth. What I want to talk about here are man-made illusions—things that are created to trick you or fantasies that are portrayed as reality.

Ever see those Barbie commercials on TV? Young girls are giggling around those beautiful, but lifeless, Barbies as if they are seeing the dolls for the first time in their lives. A big price tag "$19.99" makes you think it is such a good deal, until a faint, but hurried voice says, "$19.99 for pants and shirt only. Dolls sold separately."

Model Mania

How about those pictures of models in magazines? I always wonder why I've never bumped into one of these beauties in a supermarket or picking up their child after school. Now I realize that those perfect images are just too good to be true. Models spend hours on their make-up and take hundreds of pictures in the most flattering light to produce one or two good pictures. Then their best photo is "touched-up"—they take out zits, alter wrinkles, and create perfect complexions.

These artificial beauties represent a twisted reality. In the real world, none of my friends or their moms look like those models. However, the real people are the ones who make my life beautiful. They are the ones who care about me. They are the ones who make up the real world.

Crazy Commercials

Did you ever notice how things on TV always look better? Apples are perfectly red, toys never break, and even milk poured into a cup makes a wonderful curve. I tried to pour milk like that at home one time. I didn't make a curve... I made a mess! Now I know that there are a lot artificial things going on in the food commercials, too. People paint strawberries to make them look fresher, and they even use plastic cubes instead of ice cubes so they never melt. The funny thing is that they don't call this lying, they call it "marketing."

The important thing to wonder when you hear information is, "*Why* are they doing this?" Your nice neighbor across the street is probably bringing you cookies... to be nice. Ed McMahon is not sending you a sweepstakes entry to be nice—he wants to sell his magazines. Think about motives, and you will see magazine advertisements, lotteries, and political campaigns in a whole new way.

Then What *Is* Believing?

By now, you might agree with me that seeing is not always believing. So maybe you're wondering, "Who CAN I trust? What CAN I believe in?" Here's what *I* believe in. Everyone is different though, so your list might be very different from mine.

Believe In Your Family—I think that the underlying meaning of believing is trust. I trust my mom because I always feel that my mom loves me. I feel her unconditional love year in and year out. My mom is from mainland China where she had a hard time when she was young. Now she works in Silicon Valley as a computer engineer and she works very hard. She doesn't wear jewelry—she wears a pager and a cell phone! She enjoys working and taking care of us. She can be very strict at times, but I always know that she loves me no matter what. I'm sure you have someone in your family that you can trust, too.

Believe In Your Teachers—There is a Chinese saying, "It takes ten years to plant a tree, but it takes one hundred years to cultivate a person." To me, teachers are the gardeners of human beings. I cannot imagine what I would be like without teachers in my life.

Believe In Noble Causes—I think that we should believe in good causes and follow noble ideas. You might think that I hate every single ad on TV or in magazines. That isn't true. I was once deeply touched by an ad from the Red Cross. It simply says, "We help. Will you?" The ad is powerful because it is advocating the right thing. We should make every moment count because we can make a difference.

Believe In Yourself—This one is the most important. Some of us are born privileged, while some are under-privileged. Some are born pretty, some plain. Some are smart, some are slow. But no one is born successful, and no one is born with great accomplishments. We bear the ultimate responsibility for what our future is going to be like. No one else can make you what you want to be. No one else can keep you from what you can be.

A Girl's Web World

Beverly Reynolds, age 11

✄ Hobbies: *writing, working out, reading, hiking, drawing*

☹ Pet peeve: *when people chew with their mouths open*

✿ Dream: *to be a writer or an archaeologist*

The Internet

The Internet has always been something I've liked. On it you can chat, surf, play games, and get info. It gives you help on homework, fashion advice, and even hints about the crush of the century. In fact, you can do pretty much anything on the Internet. Intrigued? Read on!

And The Internet Is WHAT???

Surprisingly, most people who use the Internet don't really know what it is! I didn't, until I did a little research. Did you know that the Internet is not the same as the World Wide Web? See, the World Wide Web is pretty much just a bunch of sites (ya know, when you type in www.whatever.com and an awesome page shows up on the screen). But the Internet is a bunch of different things: e-mail, chatrooms, and, yes, sites. So the Internet is the World Wide Web, plus a whole lot more.

Are You Ready For This?

I wrote this chapter because I feel that most girls don't know as much about the Net as they should. They may look for a site on fashion, and end up in a chatroom about water polo. But maybe you're different. If you wonder about your skills, take my guaranteed fool-proof COMPUTER READINESS TEST... or C.R.T. Don't feel bad if you don't do well because it won't hurt your G.P.A. You're reading this chapter to learn more, anyway. **Write your answers on a separate piece of paper.**

The C.R.T. (Computer Readiness Test)

1) You are cruising the Net when a full-color advertisement for pickled pigs' feet appears on the screen. You...

   (A) try not to hurl as you look for the "Order Later" icon on the screen.

   (B) look frantically for the "X" in the corner of the screen and when you can't find it, you start panicking.

   (C) can't remember how to use a mouse, so you are forced to shut down the computer.

2) You see someone you know in a chatroom. You...

   (A) jump up and down excitedly, then try to chat, but... too late. The person has already left.

   (B) instant/private message him or her.

   (C) talk in the room openly about your secret crush, but don't bother to check the other people's profiles first—turns out half your classmates were watching every word you typed!!

3) You look for a Web site about snow boarding by...

   (A) e-mailing everyone you know, asking them to recommend one.

   (B) checking out snow boarding chatrooms, trying to dig information out of the people there.

   (C) go to Net search and type in "snow boarding."

4) When you check out a great site about orangutans, you click on one of the links. All of a sudden you find yourself on a site about fly-fishing in the Pacific Northwest. You...

   (A) don't worry. You know that you can click the "back" button and get to the orangutan site again.

   (B) type in the address of another site that you like and go explore there.

   (C) sit at the computer desk, begging the computer to help you.

5) You think a mouse is...

   (A) a little thing that goes "click."

   (B) a cute little fuzzy thing that goes "squeak."

   (C) a bird.

SCORING!

1)	A. 3	B. 2	C. 1
2)	A. 2	B. 3	C. 1
3)	A. 1	B. 2	C. 3
4)	A. 3	B. 2	C. 1
5)	A. 3	B. 2	C. 1

12-15 points: You are doing great!!

Ahhh... you've already been to the wonderful world of WWW! You know what to do, but it never hurts to know a few more things. Read on for great sites to visit.

8-11 points: Getting there... slowly...

You have a pretty good understanding of the Internet, but you still need a little help. OK, maybe a LOT of help!! But that's why you're reading this chapter!!

5-7 points: You might need a little help...

When it comes to computers, you are in trouble!! You may not really know much about computers, but you have the right attitude about learning more. This chapter will help you get started.

You And Your E-Mail

E-mail may be the most important thing you'll ever discover on the Net. It lets you contact your buds, even if they live in another state or country. You type it like a letter, but it costs less than calling them, and is faster than regular mail. Pretty amazing, huh? Hints: after you're done writing the e-mail, remember to hit SEND or it's not going anywhere. Make sure you think about what you write, though, because once you send it, it's GONE, and they *will* read it!

If you have AOL be prepared for a lot of junk e-mail. My friend Gina once received a junk e-mail for porno. Sick, huh? Luckily she didn't see anything. Still, she was a little shaken afterwards.

What can you do about this problem?

1) Tell your parents about the e-mail.

2) Write down the address and write to them, telling them never to send anything like that again.

3) E-mail AOL, telling them about the offending e-mail, and asking them to do something about it.

Ta da! That should take care of those bad e-mails.

Chats And Rats And All Of That

Chatrooms are an important part of Internet life. They help you meet new people and have fun! Of course, there are also bad things in chatrooms. Some people are sick, rude, or just plain not nice. They may use bad language or ask you private questions to embarrass you. How can you tell the good from the bad? You can follow these Simple Chatroom Rules:

1) Never give out your full name, home address, or phone number, even to a "friend."

2) Never download anything without a parent's permission.

3) If someone asks you a private question that you feel uncomfortable with, don't respond. Instead, quickly leave the chatroom.

4) If someone nonchalantly pushes a product a little too hard, be aware that they are probably selling something.

See? The rules aren't too tough!

Chat  Fun!

These are just little symbols that I created on my keyboard. You can use them to communicate with friends in a speedy and funny way. Have fun trying to make some on your own!

<———————	ARROW
@~~}~~~	ROSE
@@@@@@@ :-)	MARGE SIMPSON
;-)	WINK
:-)	HAPPY
=0)	GOOFY HAPPY
:-P	YUCK!
>:(	MAD
:- *	KISS
=0(	GOOFY SAD
:-0	SURPRISED
=0B	GOOFY BUCKTEETH
LOL	= LAUGHING OUT LOUD
TTFN	= TA TA FOR NOW
AFK	= AWAY FROM KEYBOARD
BTK	= BACK TO KEYBOARD
BRB	= BE RIGHT BACK

URLs  And You

Many people don't know what Uniform Resource Locators (URLs) are. The truth is that URLs are simple things! In fact, you've probably already used one. URLs are the addresses you type in when you are on the World Wide Web (like www.anything.com) and a page shows up.

Search The Net!

If you have a project or report due, or you just want some info, the Web is the place to look. You can find all the Web sites that have a specific word on their page! There are many different ways to do this. Whether you have Netscape, Internet Explorer, or AOL, the best way to search the Net is to use a search engine. Here's what to do:

1) Go to the Internet.

2) Type one of the following search engines into the search box:
   - altavista.digital.com
   - www.excite.com
   - www.lycos.com
   - www.infoseek.com
   - www.webcrawler.com
   - www.yahoo.com

   Try different search engines—they can all find different types of information!

3) Once you're in the search engine you want, type in the subject you are looking for, and you should get tons of cool information!

A Few of My Favorite Sites

Rating System:

**** = Cream of the Crop *** =GREAT ** = Worthy * = OK

www.purple-moon.com

Awesome site! Purple-Moon is a software company that makes software just for girls, such as "Rockett's New School," "Rockett's Tricky Decision," and "Secret Paths in the Forest." Even if you've never played the games, it's a cool site where you can meet friends, send mail, collect treasures, and much, MUCH more! Rating: ****

www.teenwish.com

This is the site for all those little goodies in magazines. You know, the mail-order things like tee shirts, lip gloss, earrings, stickers, pens, and all of that? Yep, that's Teen Wish. Cool prices, too! Rating: ***

www.bluemountainarts.com

This is a great site because it has greeting cards that you can e-mail to your best buds. All the cards are animated and some of them are even musical, so when you view the card, a song starts to play on your computer! Rating: ****

www.girlslife.com

This site is the Web sister to the print magazine *Girl's Life*. You can make CyberPals (that's a pen pal on the Internet), read about the latest software for girls, check out articles about everything from fashion to Kool-Aid, and get a few laughs in the Last Laff. There's a lot of information at this site, and it's just for girls! Rating: ***

www.thekiss.com

Yes, I know it sounds kind of mushy, but this is actually a great site for girls. The coolest feature of this site is that you can send e-mail "kisses" to your friends and family. One of my favorites is the French kiss—complete with twirly moustache and beret! Rating: ****

www.frominsideout.com

A great site because it reviews five new web sites a week! The links are always working and it's very family-oriented! Plus, I also write the reviews for the kid's sites. Rating: ***

www.girlzone.com

This site is really cool! You can chat, take quizzes, and read articles about girl stuff. You can also get homework help and learn about people from different countries. This site will keep you busy for a long time, and your parents may have to pry you off the computer! Rating: ****

www.urigeller.com

This site is about Uri Geller, the man most famous for bending spoons with his mind. Read all about psychic stuff and test your psychic abilities by playing a game where you get 20 chances to find 40 hidden items. Rating: ***

www.newmoon.org

This Web magazine is written for girls and by girls. They pick a theme and have girls submit entries of poetry, stories, or real-life adventures. The editorial board is made up of girls who pick out what to put on the site. You can Ask Luna if you have personal questions, and read what advice others have about your dilemmas. Rating: ***

Keirsey.com (there is no www in front of this address)

This site has a test you can take to find out your personality type. It also tells you what kind of personality types famous people have. It is fun to see if you and your friends match up. Rating: ***

www.bigtop.com

This site is especially good for the younger crowd. You'll find circus lingo, learn how to make arts and crafts, and try out recipes having to do with the circus. Rating: **

www.2meta.com/april-fools

You no longer have to wait until April to play these jokes on your friends. Lots and lots of funny, strange, practical jokes! Rating: ***

www.teleport.com/~jleon

Lots of slime. This site is, undoubtedly, about slime. Perfect for
when you're babysitting. It'll keep them entertained! And, you'll probably find yourself reading over their shoulders!! Rating: **

The Internet is getting bigger and bigger every day. It's a part of
the future that will affect everyone. It is also a great way to meet people and learn about things. Don't be afraid to just get on and
explore...you might become addicted!!

📖 **Publisher's Note:** *At the time of publication, these sites and
addresses were current. Because the Web changes quickly, content
or addresses may not be correct. Sorry!*

Sweet Dreams: Unlocking Their Secret Meaning

Sarah Stillman, age 14

⚞ Hobbies: *soccer, lacrosse, dancing, singing, reading*
📖 Heroes: *Eleanor Roosevelt and Mia Hamm* ☹ Pet peeve: *when girls play dumb to impress boys* ❀ Dream: *to be an author who inspires people*

How I Started Doing The Dream Thing

When I was twelve, I started having strange and scary nightmares that I was being chased down a flight of stairs. I had no idea what these dreams were signaling, or even if they meant anything at all. I decided to find out. After visiting the library on several occasions and reading through tons of intriguing dream books, I started to develop a better understanding of my dreams. Eventually, I was able to see why I was having these nightmares: I was feeling vulnerable and insecure about myself at school.

Remembering and writing about my nightmares was the first step towards making them go away. Now I am not only nightmare-free, but I actually look forward to my dream time when I can be anyone, do anything, and go anywhere!

This chapter was created especially for girls who want to discover the meaning of their dreams, but aren't quite sure how to start. Good luck and have fun with the dreams that rest under your pillow tonight!

What Are Dreams?

Did you know that just like eating and breathing, the human body needs to dream? So if you're one of those people who insists that you don't dream at all—think again. You dream every night, even if you can't remember your dreams. Although there is some conflict over the exact reason, most scientists agree that we dream to:

- ☾ release energy that we tried to hold in during the day. (Like maybe you pretended that your feelings weren't hurt when a friend was mean to you.)
- ☾ bring previously unnoticed or unrecognized skills to our attention. (Did you ever think about trying out for water polo?)
- ☾ work through our problems and think about solutions that were successful in the past.

What Dreams Have Done

People have been interested in dreams since the beginning of time. Did you know that many famous inventions, works of literature, and scientific theories were inspired by dreams? Maybe you didn't think dreams had so much importance. Well, here are some examples of the things dreams have brought us:

- ☾ The first dream interpretation book was created by Egyptians in 1300 BC!
- ☾ Albert Einstein developed his theory of relativity through a dream he had as a teenager.
- ☾ You've probably heard the story of Frankenstein by Mary Shelley. But did you know it was inspired by a dream?
- ☾ Many famous artists and authors claim that dreams have influenced their work. Salvador Dali, Anne Rice, Samuel Coleridge, and Stephen King all tie many of their greatest works to dreams!

What Is REM Sleep?

Most dreams take place in a certain kind of sleep called Rapid Eye Movement (REM) sleep. REM sleep starts about 90 minutes after you fall asleep, and continues in more frequent cycles as sleep progresses. This is the stage of sleep when anything can happen: your hamster can talk, your baby brother can tap dance, and you can fly, float, and defy all rules of gravity. In other words, you are dreaming.

Most people have between three and six dreams a night, each lasting a little longer than the one before. Your first dream may last only 10 minutes, while your final dream may last as long as 45 minutes. Even though we have about 500,000 dreams in our lifetime, it is estimated that we remember only five percent of them!

So What Do They Mean?

Very few of us realize that our dreams can unlock solutions to our problems! I had the chance to interview Carol Kurtz Walsh, who is a psychotherapist, artist, and dream expert. She told me, "Dreams are a great way to access your inner self. They're a way to learn about who you are, what you want, and what your values are. They can help us become unique individuals separate from our family and friends."

It's about time we started paying attention to the enormous power of dreams to heal our emotions, and work through our hopes and fears. "Dreams are a source of your own power... not physical power, but goddess, feminine power," continues Ms. Kurtz Walsh.

A Dream Journal

There is one absolute, definite, guaranteed key to becoming a dream expert: KEEP A DREAM JOURNAL!!! Here are the seven steps to start you on a dream journey you'll never forget:

1) First, buy a dream journal. It can be plain or fancy, whichever you prefer. Place your journal, along with a pen, beside your bed.

2) Before you go to sleep, turn to a fresh page in your journal and make some notes about your day, and anything that might be bothering you. Repeat out loud, "I will remember my dreams."

3) When you wake up, immediately try to remember any dreams you had, and write them down in your notebook.

4) Date your dreams, and give each of them a title. Try to summarize each dream in a few sentences beneath the title. Always record your dreams in the present tense (Ex: I am running) instead of the past tense (Ex: I ran) so that you can use the past tense for events that actually happened as flashbacks in the dream.

5) When you write about your dreams, be sure to include detailed information about what you saw, where you were, colors and sounds that you remember. Don't worry if you can't remember the whole dream. As you write, more of the dream will probably come back to you. Also, don't worry about spelling or grammar.

6) If you wake up in the night with a dream, or you don't have time to record your dream when you get up in the morning, at least try to write down a few key words or phrases that will help you remember later.

7) On the opposite page of your journal, write how you felt when you woke up from the dream, and anything in real life that the dream might relate to.

*Note: Don't be discouraged if you can't remember your dreams at first. As you practice, slowly your dreams will become easier to recall.

Getting ❀ The Message

Now it's time for the fun, exciting, and rewarding part of your dream work... figuring them out! Dreams can appear incredibly strange and random, but if you search hard enough, most of them contain important messages.

There are several different approaches you can use to interpret your dreams. Here is one example: once I had a dream that I was at a piano recital. When it was my turn to play a song, I realized that I didn't know my piece at all! My piano teacher called an intermission so that I could learn the piece, but there wasn't enough time. I finally got up the courage to ask if I could sing a song instead. My teacher agreed.

The first thing to do is list all the important symbols in the dream. So I wrote down: piano, singing, piano teacher, and intermission. Next, I brainstormed about each symbol. My list looked like this:

- ☾ Piano: music, unfamiliar to me
- ☾ Singing: beautiful, fun, familiar
- ☾ Piano teacher: kind, chubby, understanding
- ☾ Intermission: a break from work

And The Answer Is...

After this, I thought about my overall feeling in the dream, which was anxiety and insecurity at first, and then relief that I could sing instead of play piano. Finally, I put all the symbols together to find the meaning of the dream. I was on Spring break (or "intermission") at the time, and so I think my dream was telling me that instead of always trying to work (memorizing the piano piece), I should let myself have fun (singing). My dream was telling me to relax and enjoy my vacation!

Recurring Dreams

When interpreting your dreams, it is important to look at each dream separately, but you should also pay attention to connections between different dreams. Sometimes you might have several different dreams that contain repeated symbols. You might even have the same dream over and over. This is called a recurring dream.

Q: Help! I keep having a recurring dream that I'm late for a major exam at school. When I get there, I suddenly realize that I completely forgot to prepare!

A: Don't worry... in fact, be happy! Recurring dreams are windows into our souls! They are often the very best dreams to analyze. The "test worry" dream is a common one, and probably has a fairly simple interpretation. It could represent something in your life that you've procrastinated or need to prepare for. You may be entering a real-life situation in which you have been asked to do something you feel unqualified for.

Figuring Them Out

Don't just ignore or dismiss your recurring dreams by saying, "Oh, I've had that boring old dream again for the thousandth time." Try not to be afraid of your recurring dreams, even if they force you to face up to something which is scary, sad, or frightening. Any recurring dream needs special work and attention.

First, you must confront your dream and accept the fact that it is definitely trying to tell you something about yourself. Next, write down your repetitive dream in even greater detail than you might normally record your dreams. The more you study your dream, the clearer it will become. You might notice that nightmares tend to disappear when you acknowledge and attempt to understand them. You might also discover a certain pattern emerging. For example, your dream might occur whenever you have a big math test coming up.

Nightmares

With recurring nightmares, you may wish to look closely at one of the symbols in your dream and ask why it scares you. Another thing you can do is imagine yourself going through the dream again, but this time either change the outcome or add a character (such as a family member) to protect you.

Sweet  Dreams

If you want to encourage happy dreaming, then you might want to start some special bedtime traditions. Near bedtime, drink warm, soothing drinks such as chamomile tea instead of caffeinated sodas. Also, try to avoid large meals after 9 p.m. Your before-bed ritual could include taking a warm bath or writing in a journal. Finally, keep your bedroom slumber-friendly, with a comfortable temperature, low noise level, and dim light to help you sleep.

Having Fun With Your Dreams

Once you feel in control of your dreams, there are lots of fun things you can do with them. Try a few of these clever dream ideas!

1) **Dream Club:** You might be surprised at all the neat dream opportunities out there. Look around your neighborhood. If you live in a big town, there is probably a dream workshop or dream group that you can join. If not, get some friends together and start your very own dream club, with you as president, of course! It can be great fun to share your dreams with friends.

2) **Dreamy Art:** As you know, dreams are great sources of inspiration for many inventors, writers, and artists. Why not create some "dreamworks" of your own? Once you do, you can bind them together in a dreamy art book to keep private or to let friends and family enjoy.

3) **Dream Incubation:** Do you have a particularly difficult decision coming up? Are you looking for a solution to an especially complex predicament? Here's a simple secret that was used by ancient Egyptian, Greek, Roman, and Chinese people for thousands of years and can still work for you today: dream incubation. This is where you search for answers in your dreams. To start, write down everything you can think of concerning a particular problem or situation. Then, before you go to bed, ask your dream for information regarding this topic. When you awake in the morning, analyze the night's dreams carefully. They just might contain the answers you're searching for!

Dream Symbols

Many objects in dreams symbolize feelings or experiences from real life. You can use a dream dictionary to find out possible explanations for the symbols in your dreams. Ms. Kurtz Walsh told me that "there are no right or wrong ways to interpret dream symbols." Therefore, you have to be careful to think about your own feelings when you analyze your dreams. For example, not all people are scared of snakes. In fact, some people think of snakes as beautiful, healing creatures. So snakes can't possibly have the same meaning in all dreams. Remember to apply your own feelings when you use the following Dream Dictionary!

Dream Dictionary

Here are common dream symbols and what they may represent:

Airplane: You're probably feeling on top of the world—independent and confident. If you dream about a crash, it could be saying that your hopes about something recently took a nose dive.

Being chased: This could show that you are trying to escape from something, not wanting to face up to something, or that something is "catching up" with you.

Drowning: Are you feeling helpless or in over your head? You could be experiencing emotional overload.

Falling: This could represent a loss of confidence or a feeling of helplessness about something. It's possible you fear being rejected by important people in your life.

Fire: This could symbolize love, frustration, anger, or any other strong and "burning" emotion. Or maybe the fire is trying to shed light on something you haven't noticed?

Flying: A wonderful symbol! Probably indicates joyful feelings, a sense of freedom, or confidence about an achievement.

Running: What are you running away from? It may be you're trying to escape responsibilities, such as studying for that huge exam, or you may be fleeing from painful emotions you don't want to face.

More About Dreams

If you want to learn more about dreams, here are some good books you might want to read:

- *Cloud Nine: A Dreamer's Dictionary*, by Sandra A. Thomson
- *Dreams Can Help: A Journal Guide to Understanding Your Dreams and Making Them Work for You*, by Jonni Kincher
- *The Secret Language of Dreams*, by David Fontana
- *Dreaming*, by Derek Parker

Once you start your journal and get on the path to learning from your dreams, you'll probably be hooked for life. Just remember to have fun and trust your own instincts. Sweet dreams!

Losing A Loved One

Whitney Alexander, age 12

✧ Hobbies: *the martial art of poekoelan, collecting Beanie Babies™ and key chains* ☺ Pet peeve: *when people say, "I have the same thing, except it's different."* ❀ Dream: *to be an architect*

Sydney Boling, age 12

✧ Hobbies: *reading, soccer, basketball, piano* ☺ Pet peeve: *when people say, "Guess what? Oh, never mind."* ❀ Dream: *to become the editor of a magazine*

Our Experiences

We chose to write about losing a loved one because we both had to deal with this experience. We realized that there are not many books that help girls deal with this. We think it is important to write about this so that we can help other girls who are going through this.

Whitney: My brother died two years before I was born. Tragically, he was killed by a gunshot when he was 10 years old. I found out that I had had a brother when I was very young. I sometimes feel sad when I talk about him and sometimes I cry. Even though I didn't know him, I still feel sad. It is sort of strange knowing that I had a brother I never knew.

Sydney: When I was 5 years old my mom first got breast cancer. She went through chemotherapy treatment, and they thought she was cured. When I was 10 my mom's cancer returned. She tried many different treatments, but about a year ago she died. I was prepared for her death, but that didn't make it easier. During her illness, I went to a counselor who helps kids with parents who have cancer.

Everyone feels differently about losing a loved one. In this chapter we are not telling you how to feel or act, we are just giving you ideas.

Talking With Acquaintances

You'll probably notice that when someone you know dies, people try to talk to you. You may not feel comfortable talking to them, so just chat politely. You don't need to get personal if you don't want to.

Sydney: I remember at my mom's memorial service that a lot of my mom's old friends tried to talk to me. I felt embarrassed and uncomfortable. When they asked me questions, I didn't go into much detail—I just sort of nodded my head politely.

Whitney: When people want to talk to me about my brother I am usually open about my feelings. Usually when people do that they are just trying to be nice, so you should try to be polite.

Talking With Family And Friends

Sydney: While my mother was dying I was very sad and depressed. I didn't talk to my friends about it very much. It's not that I felt uncomfortable talking to them. It's just that I had to deal with my mother's problem at home, so while I was at school I didn't want to talk about it. I just wanted a break. I handled the problem in a way that suited me. Now, after my mother's death, I am pretty open with my friends and I am glad to have friends who are such good listeners.

Whitney: When people ask if I have a brother I always say that I had a brother, but he died two years before I was born. Sometimes when I am talking about him I just start crying. I am really open about his death with other people because it is easier for me to deal with it that way.

Time Off

When you lose a loved one, you may need to take some time off from school before you feel comfortable there again. Some may only need a few days off, while others may need a few weeks. Give yourself the space you need, but don't fall behind—your loved one wouldn't want that.

Surviving The Funeral

Funerals can be very depressing. Funerals are usually very sad because people talk about how sad it is that your loved one died. It might make the funeral better if you try to think about their life and the good times you had with them instead of focusing on their death and how sad it is.

You may feel scared about going to the funeral, but we think that you should still try to go. Memorials and funerals are definitely uncomfortable, but they honor your loved one. It helps your heart heal a little when you see all the people who have loved them. You may regret it later if you don't go. However, some people really are frightened of funerals, so you need to make your own decision.

Will People Ever Treat Me Normally Again?

Yes. Eventually people will start to treat you normally again, but for a little while they will treat you like you are very fragile. When people do this, they are just trying to show you that they care.

Remember Their Birthday

We think that it is a good idea to remember your loved one's birthday or the anniversary of their death. This is a good way to get family and friends together to remember your loved one. On the anniversary of my mother's death my father, my mom's friends, and I are going to a special place in a public garden that has a bench in my mom's name. I think occasions like this are a good way to share your memories and love for the person.

Helping The Hurt

Losing someone is hard, especially when it's someone that is such a big part of your life. You probably never imagined that they wouldn't always be around. When you don't have them any more, it is very hard to get used to. For a while things will seem like they will never be normal again. Your life will feel empty, because something is missing. Here are some activities that are helpful for people who are grieving:

Six Helpful Steps

1) **A journal** is a very good way to express your feelings. While you are writing you don't need to be specific. You know what you are thinking about and it doesn't need to come out perfectly on paper. Sometimes this is better than talking to someone because you won't be interrupted. It's a nice, secret place to put your thoughts.

2) Go to **independent counseling**. Don't think about the stereotype of a psychologist. Counselors are people who are trained to help you feel better. They can help you talk about how you feel. You could go to a school counselor or a special counselor at a doctor's office.

3) Go to an organized **group counseling** session. This is counseling with other people who are in a similar situation. It's comforting to talk to people who know what you're going through. By talking to people, you may get some good input on how to deal with your pain.

4) It's always a good idea to **have a special place** where you can be alone. I know that sometimes when I have a particularly bad day I like to be alone where nobody can talk to me. You could go to a closet, the basement, or a tree house—anywhere you can be by yourself.

5) It's good to **have a pet around** to talk to. It may sound a little strange, but I think it is really helpful. Sometimes when you are sad it is comforting just to talk to a pet and touch its soft fur.

Studies show that petting an animal lowers your stress level and helps lift sadness!

6) **Talk about your emotions.** Find a friend, counselor, teacher, or family member you can talk to. Bottling up your feelings can result in outrage and depression. You will be surprised how much better you will feel when you talk things out.

Helping A Friend Who Has Lost A Loved One

If you have a friend who has recently lost someone close to them, you may be worried about how to help. There are many things you can do to be a supportive friend. Here are some questions and answers to help you help her:

Q: Is it okay to talk to your friend about their loved one who died?

A: Yes it is okay, but you may find it difficult to talk to a friend who has gone through this. Ask her if she wants to talk, and if she does, then listen. Let her do most of the talking and don't interrupt. If she doesn't want to talk, then don't pressure her. Be patient. Eventually your friend may want to talk, but if she never decides to, then just show your love.

Q: Can you ask how the person died?

A: We actually like it when people ask about what happened to the deceased. It shows that they care enough to ask, but be sensitive to your friend's feelings.

Q: If a member of my friend's family dies, how should I treat her?

A: Don't feel shy or scared—she is still your friend, she's just going through a difficult time. But also don't treat her like nothing has happened. Be there if she wants to talk, but otherwise, just be her friend.

Conclusion

We hope that these suggestions help you. Having a loved one die can be one of the hardest things you ever have to deal with. Just remember that you will get through it. Eventually the pain will get better. You'll never forget your loved one, but you will be able to face the future with hope again.

 ## Losing A Grandparent

Courtney Moffett-Bateau, age 12

❀ Dream: *to drive an original Mustang convertible*

Many girls experience the loss of a grandparent. My grandfather died last year, and it was a very sad time for me and my family. I want to share what I learned with other girls who are going through this.

My grandfather was sick for several months, and he had to go to the hospital. Luckily I lived close by so I was able to visit him and tell him how much I loved him. If your grandparent is in the hospital, visit them and give them love and hope. If you are not able to visit them, make them a card or story and mail it to them. Call them on the phone and tell them that you love them.

Communicate Your Feelings

When a grandparent dies suddenly, you may not be able to tell them good-bye. This may be very difficult, but it might help you to write them a letter expressing your feelings. Even though you won't be able to send the letter, you will still be able to express your feelings for them.

When your grandparent dies, it is very important that you talk about your feelings with someone you love. When I was sad about my grandfather, I talked about it with my mother and we found out that we had many of the same feelings. It helped both of us share our memories.

Support Your Parents

Remember that when your grandparent dies, your parents probably hurt even more than you do because they have lost a parent. Your mom or dad will probably be really sad. You could help them by making them a card or helping around the house. They will probably want to have some time alone, so be sensitive to their feelings. If you share your memories about the grandparent with your mom or dad, they will feel better knowing that you care about the loved one, too.

 # It's Okay To Pamper Your Parents

Rachael Bentsen, age 12

❀ Dream: *to overcome all of life's obstacles*

Do your parents sometimes drive you crazy?! I used to feel that way, too, but then I had a experience that made me never want to take them for granted again. Last summer my mom started having problems with her leg. She went to the doctors and they found that she had a brain tumor bigger than a lemon. They had to do a very serious surgery. Luckily, she survived and is doing fine now. While she was going through this I realized how much I love her. Here are some things that I learned about appreciating your parents:

Eight Ways to Appreciate Your Parents

1) Pay attention to what they are saying so they know you actually listen.

2) Support them and everything they do because they support you.

3) Learn from them because they have more experience than you do.

4) Be there for them when they need you most (they have bad days, too).

5) Always speak kindly about them to other people.

6) Tell them that you love them—a lot!

7) Work hard to resolve conflict; every parent hates fights.

8) Show that you appreciate all they do for you.

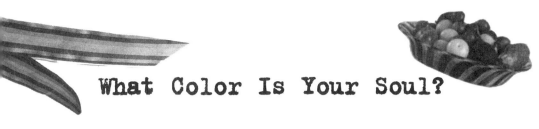

What Color Is Your Soul?

Dena Gordon, age 15

✂ Hobbies: *sports, computers* ☹ Pet peeve: *when people don't respect my privacy* 🖘 Hero: *my mom* ✿ Dream: *to make the world a better place*

Every day there is vibrant, amazing color all around us! Sometimes we forget to notice emerald green grass, a brilliant orange and pink sunset, or the bright yellow of a daffodil. In the homes we live in, the clothing we wear, and the natural world, color is a huge part of our lives.

My Color Heritage

I began learning about color when I very young, because it is very important to my family. My grandfather is a painter-decorator. He mixes a rainbow of colors, and then helps people to coordinate their walls with the rest of their houses. My mother is a professional color analyst, which means that she helps people discover the power of colors in their life. So now you can see that I have grown up with a lot of "color heritage." I knew shades of blueberry, strawberry, apricot, and peach before I knew how to write my name!

The Colors That Are You

When a child is born, they are born with their own unique combination of colors. This color impression stays with a person throughout their whole life! The natural harmony of a person is made up of the color of the skin, the eyes and the hair. When I was 2 years old, my mother brought me to her color teacher for my color analysis. She told my mom which colors were part of my palette. By now you may be wondering what YOUR colors are! Well, you're in luck, because you are going to get your own color analysis today!

So what is the color of your soul?
We can use your eye as a window to see.
Embark upon this wonderful journey—
I'll take you along with me.

The Colors Of The Seasons

Color analysts use the four seasons to describe people. In nature, each season brings its own atmosphere and colors. Just like the seasons, each individual fits into one of those same categories. The first thing you have to decide is: which season are you? Although the following descriptions will help you guess what season you are, if you want to know for sure, you need to see a color analyst who is trained to read you from the inside out.

Autumn Girl: The autumn girl has skin and hair coloring like the warm, rich earth colors of fall. Autumns are often girls with brown hair with gold or red highlights, and they usually have brown, green, or hazel eyes. Redheads with brown eyes are also autumns. Many girls of Native-American or Indian background are autumns, especially if they have warm skin tones. Autumns look best in warm, fall colors like brown, gold, orange, rust, peaches, teals, and forest green. Famous autumns: Kate Winslett and Julia Roberts.

Winter Girl: When winter comes, suddenly everything is in pure contrast. The winter girl sparkles with the vivid icy colors of a frosty day. Winters have cool skin that is olive, black, milky white, or pink. Many African-American and Asian girls are winters, particularly if their hair has blue-black highlights. Many winters have dark hair, light skin, and icy blue or gray eyes. Winters look great in bold colors and sharp contrasts. They can wear true white, black, bold red, hot pink, bright blue, green, and purple. Famous winters: Elizabeth Taylor and Toni Braxton.

Spring Girl: Water-washed and sun-drenched, the spring girl looks like an open-faced flower: clear. She has warm coloring, and a very delicate look to her face. Often springs have peachy skin, light blue or blue-green eyes, and blonde or blondish-brown hair. Redheads with blue eyes are usually springs too. Springs are wonderful in warm, clear colors like peach, gold, light brown, green-blues, and orange-reds, and violet. Famous springs: Marilyn Monroe and Uma Thurman.

Summer Girl: When the bright shiny sun of summer comes out, it bakes all the bright colors of spring and begins to make them subtle and muted. Summers glow in the soft colors of the sea and sky with cool, blue undertones. Summers have pink or yellow-tinted skin, with blonde, light brown, or ash-colored hair. Summer girls usually have blue eyes, but they can occasionally have green or hazel eyes too. Summers shine in all the soft pastels and cool colors: powdery blue, pink, and lavender. Famous summers: Kim Basinger and Alicia Silverstone.

The Power Of Color

Now that you have a good idea of what season you might be, use the colors of your season to bring you "color power!" Color is a mood, a feeling, and an emotion. Have you ever noticed after wearing something the whole day, you feel like you're just not "you?" That's because you're probably not wearing your colors! Here are some color hints for you to try out. You will be amazed at the power that lies within the world of color!

Healing Colors

Did you know that when you have a cold you should wrap yourself in a cobalt blue blanket? The color will actually make you feel better.

When sick people have colorful flowers in their hospital room, it isn't just for comfort. The cheerfulness of the colors actually helps heal the person.

Mood Colors

When you want to be approachable, wear a color that matches your skin. When you want to be feminine, pinch the tip of your finger and watch your blood come up. Wear that color for great results! If you want to be relaxed, match the color of what you're wearing to the color of your eyes. Do you want to be dramatic? Wear the brightest color in your season or a red. When you want to be quiet, wear your softest color. If you are sad and moody, put on a sunshine color and brighten up your day. The term "royal purple" comes from when the monarchy wore purple cloaks and robes, so for a regal feeling wear purple.

What Your Color Says About You

Did you know that the colors you are naturally drawn to say a lot about you? Because colors are a feeling, they describe your soul. Think of your favorite color, the color that is the most you. Now look below to see what your color reveals about your soul!

+ **Rockin' Red:** Girls who love red are usually powerful and bold. They are passionate, intense, outgoing, and talkative. These are the girls who stand out in the crowd because they are lively, vibrant, and charismatic.
+ **Beautiful Blue:** If your soul is blue you are probably a dreamer. Thoughtful and introspective, you are gentle, easy-going, and sensitive. People appreciate your ability to relax and take life as it comes.
+ **Gorgeous Green:** Green girls are lovers of the earth. Your soul is full of peace, nature, balance, and harmony. You are most likely clear-headed and focused. The power of green gives you a clear direction and love for life.

- **Yummy Yellow:** Girls who love yellow are rays of sunshine. These are the excited, bright, and friendly girls who are completely full of life. You are joyful, happy-go-lucky and cheerful, but you have your calm moments, too.
- **Openly Orange:** If you are orange in your heart, you are a combination of red and yellow. Because of that you can be both introspective and intense—dramatic, energetic, and analytical. Artists are often orange, and they love being complex and flamboyant.
- **Perfectly Pink**: Pink ladies are usually optimistic and hopeful. Generous and affectionate, pink girls are true and trustworthy friends. Although you may be shy at first, once you are comfortable, you love to share your soul.
- **Passionate Purple:** Girls who love purple are a combination of red and blue. They tend to be artistic, expressive, romantic, and emotional. Purple girls can be crazy and creative, but also introspective. You are different, and you *love* to be that way!

I hope you have enjoyed this journey into the world of color. There is a lot more out there to experience, so if you want to learn more, I recommend the book *Color Style* by Carolyn Warrender. Colors are something we often take for granted, but can you imagine how boring the world would be without them? Appreciate *all* the colors in your life!

Sweet Sensations

Keila Santos, age 12

✂ Hobbies: *reading, shopping, talking with my friends*
☹ Pet peeve: *people who don't accept someone because
they're different* ▯ Heroes: *my mom and dad* ❀ Dream:
to be a famous singer or actress

Homemade Candy And Other Treats

Most girls I know love anything sweet, just like I do. Making sweets
at home is even better, though, because it can be a lot of fun, and you
can get really creative. Somehow homemade treats always taste better,
too. In this chapter you will learn how to make a few of my favorite
concoctions. Don't just stick to the rules though—imagine great varia-
tions. Make sure you ask your parents' permission before you start
because if you're like me, you will probably make a mess!

Banana Boats

This is a really fun recipe to make with friends because it is fast,
easy, and really yummy.

What You Need:

FOOD   **UTENSILS**

1 banana for each person   tin foil
1 cup peanut butter   butter knife
1 plain chocolate bar

What You Do:

1. Pre-heat oven to 450°F (230°C).
2. Take the unpeeled bananas and slit them length-wise down the
    middle to form a boat-like shape. DO NOT SLIT ALL THE WAY
    THROUGH!!!

3. Take a butter knife and spread peanut butter so that inside the banana there is a thick layer of peanut butter. Do this to all of the bananas.

4. Take the chocolate bar and break it into small pieces. Put 3-4 small pieces in each banana, on top of the peanut butter. Gently close the bananas together.

5. Now, wrap each banana by itself in tin foil and bake them in the oven for 8 to 10 minutes. Now you have banana boats!!

Dandy Rock Candy

This is a recipe for rock candy and it usually turns out to be delicious! Your first time it might not turn out perfectly, but it still tastes great!

What You Need:

FOOD	UTENSILS
4 cups (800 g) sugar	a medium-sized saucepan
1 cup (240 ml) water	a wide-necked glass jar (like a washed-out mayonnaise jar)
food coloring (optional)	3 pieces of string, each 12 inches (30 cm) long
	a new pencil

What You Do:

1. Tie the pieces of string in a knot around the pencil so that six inches hang off each side.

2. Pour the water into the saucepan. Now, pour only 2 cups (400 g) of the sugar into the pan and cook on medium heat. DO NOT LET IT BOIL!!!! Stir until all the sugar dissolves.

3. Gradually add the rest of the sugar. Stir until that sugar dissolves, too.

4. Pour the sugar water into the jar and set the prepared pencil over the jar with the strings hanging into the water.

5. Now comes the hardest part of all—waiting! Put the jar where it can sit without being disturbed for about two weeks.

6. Every other day check on it and gently, without disturbing the strings, crush the crystal that forms around the top of the sugar water. In two to four weeks break the candy out of the jar (it will be attached to the strings). You will now have some delicious rock candy.

Brazilian Pudding

This is a fantastic dessert that is very popular in Brazil. My dad is from Brazil and he says it is a very traditional dish that is served after dinner. This pudding is a bit harder than the other recipes, but once you try it you'll agree that Brazilians know a lot about food!

What You Need:

FOOD

14 oz. (420 ml) sweetened
condensed milk
14 oz. (420 ml) regular milk
(just refill the can with milk)
4 eggs
2 cups (400 g) sugar
1 cup (240 ml) water

UTENSILS

a big sauce pan
a wooden spoon
a bundt pan (a round pan with
a hole in the middle)

What You Do:

1. Pre-heat oven to 350°F (180°C).
2. Pour the sweetened condensed milk, the regular milk, and the eggs into a blender and blend for 10 minutes.
3. While the blender is going, pour the sugar into a pan. Cook on medium heat until sugar has completely melted.
4. Once sugar has melted, stand back and slowly pour the water in. Stir with wooden spoon at medium-low heat till sugar has become a thick caramel brown syrup. Pour the syrup into your bundt pan.
5. Find a large metal pan which the bundt pan fits into and pour an inch of water into it. Place the bundt pan inside the other pan. (Don't let any water get in the pudding.)

6. Now gently pour your blender mix over the sugar. Do it very gently so that you don't disturb the caramelized sugar.

7. Cover the pans with tin foil and put both pans in the oven. Cook approximately 1 hour or until a toothpick comes out clean.

8. When the pudding is done cooking, peel the tin foil off and take the bundt pan out of the water pan. Put a plate upside down onto the bundt pan. Gently flip the bundt pan over. The pudding will slide onto the plate.

9. Place the plate with the pudding into the refrigerator for about 30 minutes. Once it is completely cold, dig in and enjoy!

I hope you enjoy making and eating these recipes. They were a lot of fun to share with you. Happy cooking!!

Ten Wacky Things To Do With Chocolate Syrup

Rachel Westbrook, age 13

❀ Dream: *to be a famous accordion player or a well-known actress*

Syrup, Syrup Galore

There are so many things you can do with chocolate syrup! This isn't a joke—it's advice for people who love chocolate.

1. Dip oranges in chocolate syrup. It's a great combination. Try other fruit like strawberries and apples, too.

2. Turn chocolate into art. Paint your syrup onto a plate, and then proceed to lick it. If you feel like getting really inventive, spike your artwork with one of these: mini-marshmallows, oatmeal, coconut, or anything else you find interesting.

3. Add a bit of chocolate syrup to your orange soda. Mmm...

4. Decorate your pancakes with chocolate smiley faces, stars, spirals, Mickey Mouse, Botticelli's *Birth of Venus*—anything at all!

5. Mix something carbonated, like sparkling water or grape soda, with some chocolate syrup for a genuine chocolate soda.

6. Pour small amounts of milk-thinned chocolate syrup over cereal in the place of milk.

7. Why overlook the obvious? Chocolate syrup + milk = chocolate milk. No more lumpy, powdery crud.

8. Use chocolate syrup instead of chocolate candy bars when making s'mores over a campfire. Chocolate bars never melt anyway.

9. Get yourself a small mold or a cookie cutter and a very flat plate. Set the mold on the plate, pour syrup into the mold, and freeze it. Voila! Your own chocolate shapes.

10. Be creative. Use your mind. Come up with your own uses for this magnificent confection. Chocolate syrup is an extremely useful tool. Just think: where would we be without it?

Sidestepping Sticky Situations

Briana Lovell, age 12

✂ Hobbies: *outdoor and indoor soccer, basketball, piano*

✎ Favorite classes: *math and phys. ed.* ☺ Pet peeve: *when teachers say things indirectly* ❀ Dream: *to live in Europe*

DeAngela Venable, age 12

✎ Favorite class: *math* ☺ Pet peeve: *when people call me "nappy-headed"* ♫ Hero: *my mom* ❀ Dream: *to be rich*

Risky Business

There are times when it is good to take a risk, and other times when it is best to avoid a situation. If you take a dangerous risk, you could expose yourself to injury or hazard. We want to talk about some of the difficult risks that are out there for girls today. Sometimes it is hard to know how to avoid these risks and keep yourself safe.

We decided to write about avoiding risky situations partly because of problems that we see around us and partly because we are learning to say "no" in health class. Writing this has helped us to realize how important these issues are.

Peer Pressure

Sometimes your peers try to pressure you into doing things that you don't want to do. Whether it's about drugs, boys, or parties, it can be very hard to withstand pressure. However, it is important that you know how to say "no" to your peers. If someone tries to pressure you, look the person in the eye, stand in one place, and firmly tell them, "No."

If you are moving around, fidgeting, or looking at the ground, it sends a message that you are not really sure about your answer. You have to make sure that the person understands the first time that you really mean "no." Don't give in to the pressure just so you can fit in. Don't give reasons why you don't want to do it, because then they will keep arguing. It's really difficult to argue with a firm "no."

Smoking

Briana: I learned a lot about the results of taking risks from my grandpa. He died last year from the effects of smoking and drinking too much alcohol over a long period of time. He had emphysema and lung cancer from smoking and cirrhosis of the liver from drinking. About a year before he died he stopped smoking, but it was too late. We have a lot of friends who have also lost relatives and friends from the effects of smoking, taking drugs, or drinking.

Some kids start smoking because they see grown-ups smoking, but the risks just aren't worth it. Smoking ruins your lungs and is very addictive. You have go through a very difficult withdrawal process with smoking. If you are concerned about looking good, you should definitely not smoke because smoking turns your teeth yellow! Smoking makes the skin on your face age more quickly and it also makes your breath smell horrible. If your parents smoke, you need to be concerned about second-hand smoke. You could ask them to quit, but if they refuse, ask them to smoke outside.

Drugs

Drugs are a serious risk to your health, and they are also dangerous legally. If you are caught at school or by the police in possession of drugs, you could get in very serious trouble. You might be arrested or fined. One of the problems with drugs in general is that they are very addictive and very expensive. It takes lots and lots of money to keep a drug habit going.

Some of the harm caused by drugs comes from how you behave when you are high. When you are high, different drugs cause different reactions. Alcohol blurs your judgment. Hard drugs can make you drowsy, unpredictable, or violent. They are all addictive in different ways, and using them can ruin your lungs, transmit AIDS, and even kill you.

Alcohol

Drinking alcohol is a very serious problem. The majority of kids who are alcoholics start drinking as a way to deal with stress. You cannot escape your problems this way. Positive ways to deal with stress include meditation, writing, and exercise. Alcohol doesn't allow you to work through your problems, it just makes you forget for a little while. As soon as you're sober you remember them again and want to drink. This vicious cycle can lead quickly to alcoholism. If you or your friend is addicted to alcohol, it is important that you recognize it and try to get help. Briana has an uncle who was an alcoholic, but he went to AA and he has managed to stop drinking.

Reckless Driving

When you get your driver's license, you might feel like you can do anything that you want to. However, driving is a big responsibility. Not all teenagers are reckless drivers, but be careful who you drive with. Crazy driving is not a good way to impress your friends. Every year, hundreds of teens are killed in auto accidents. Never, ever, drive with someone who has been drinking.

Good Risks

There are a lot of times when taking a risk is a good idea. If you never took risks, you would never leave your home or try anything new, like roller blading. Every day you do things that may be a risk, but the chance that something bad will come of it is low enough that you are safe.

It is critical that you develop a good sense of when it is best to take a risk and when it is best to avoid a situation. Here are some questions to ask yourself about the risk to see if it's good or bad:

1) Would your parents be angry if they found out?
2) Are you really scared (sick stomach, sweaty palms, unclear thoughts) or just excited (like before a roller coaster)?
3) Is it illegal?
4) Do you really not want to do it in your heart of hearts?
5) Does it agree with what you believe in and who you are?

Sometimes keeping yourself safe will make you feel left out by your peers. If you are different, that is okay! Being unique is a very good thing. Most importantly, you have to live true to your own values.

Learn More

If you are interested in learning more about how you can overcome risk situations, we recommend these books:

☞ *Taking Charge of My Mind & Body: A Girl's Guide to Outsmarting Alcohol, Drug, Smoking, and Eating Problems* by Gladys Folkers and Jeanne Engelmann

☞ *Reviving Ophelia: Saving the Selves of Adolescent Girls* by Dr. Mary Pipher

Can Guys Be Risky?

Nancy Siv, age 13

❀ Dream: *to make a difference in our world*

Maybe you don't feel like you're ready for a relationship. If you're not, don't push yourself! Relationships can be great, but you don't need a guy to make you feel special. If you are ready

to date, don't go out with just anyone. And don't ever forget your friends and your priorities. Guys come and go, but true friendships last forever.

Bad Relationships

If you've ever seen a bad relationship, you know that dating can be a risky situation. You have to be careful who you fall for. You want to make sure that the guy you like treats you with respect. If he doesn't, he isn't worth your time. A relationship is not a game and should be taken seriously because it can affect you emotionally and physically!

Choose Wisely

It will save you a lot of time if you don't get into a bad relationship in the first place. If you know the guy is bad news, don't go for him. He isn't worth it. If he does drugs or is abusive, you should stay far away. You don't want your guy to have a bad influence on you.

Being In A Bad Relationship

No one wants to be in a bad relationship, but it does happen. There are many things that can lead up to being in a bad relationship. Usually there are warning signs:

- ✗ He insults you.
- ✗ He argues with you a lot.
- ✗ He flirts with other girls.
- ✗ He touches you in ways you don't want to be touched.
- ✗ He abuses you in any way.

These are all signs of a bad relationship. If you need to, don't be afraid to talk to someone and get help. This is not a game, and should be taken seriously.

Getting Out

Getting out of a bad relationship can be a hard thing to do. If you're going to break up with him, talk to him nicely. Gently tell him that the relationship isn't working out, and that you'd rather be friends. If that doesn't work, tell him again but more firmly. Say what you have to say, and leave. It hurts and it's hard, but believe me, you will be better off without him.

A relationship involves two people, so both people should have a say about what goes on in the relationship. Don't let him tell you what to do or when to do it. He has no right to boss you around. He doesn't rule the world and he doesn't own you. You are no one's property. It's a new era—women have equal rights in this nation. Stand up for yourself!

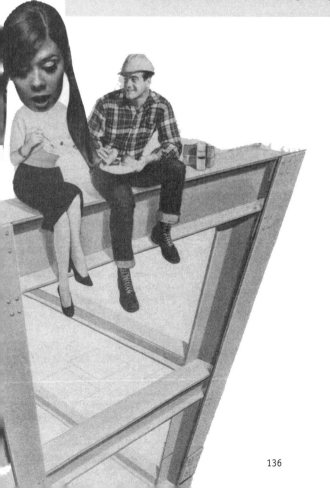

PAMPERED PETS

Taylor Borg, age 12

✄ Hobbies: *cornet, reading, soccer, basketball, playing with friends and pets* ☺ Pet peeve: *when people don't take care of their pets* ♬ Hero: *any woman who works with penguins* ✿ Dream: *to have 101 dogs and a big farm out in the country*

Loving Pets

Pets have always been a very important part of my life. My family has always had dogs and other assorted pets. My first pet that was my very own was a guinea pig named Trina. I got her when I was 3 years old. I learned a lot from having a pet of my own because it taught me about responsibility and commitment. It was also nice to have a small animal that I could hug and talk to.

Pets are a big responsibility because of all the time you have to put into taking care of them. Pets totally rely on you to feed them, exercise them, keep their homes clean, and give them love and attention. When you get a pet you make them a promise that you will always love and care for them. If you are not willing to do all this, then you are not the type of person who should get a pet. You should probably just enjoy animals at friends' houses, the zoo, or the aquarium instead.

Different types of pets need different types of care. Dogs for instance, need more time for exercise than animals like snakes. Some animals such as hamsters, are nocturnal, which means they are more awake at night than during the day. You need to choose a pet that is right for your lifestyle. If you live in an apartment or a small house, you probably should not get a large dog that will want a lot of space. A better choice might be a small dog, a cat or a small animal that can live in a cage.

Top Ten Ways To Convince Your Parents To Get A Pet

Lauren Guida, age 10

❀ Dream: *to be a gymnastics star*

So, you want to get a pet, but your parents are skeptical? Here are ten ways to sway them!

1) **Responsibility!** It means everything to parents. So promise to help feed the animal, keep it clean, and play with it.

2) **Compromise.** If your parents don't want a certain animal, get something that both you and your parents will like.

3) **Money.** If your parents are worried about paying for the animal, offer to help pay with some of your own money.

4) **Be gleeful.** Let your parents know how happy your pet will make you, and how much you will love it.

5) **A friend.** Point out that pets are great company. If you're lonely, they'll make you feel safe and protected. If you're bored, you can count on your pet to play with you.

6) **A teacher.** You can also mention that pets teach people how to be responsible, gentle, and loving.

7) **Photo hints**. Cut out pictures of your pet-to-be from a magazine and plaster them all over your house.

8) **Be a pet sitter!** Ask to watch someone else's pet for a few days, and make sure it's a good experience for your parents.

9) **Become the local expert** on your pet. Get books, ask friends, and get pamphlets from the humane society. Then casually mention some of your new knowledge when your parents are listening.

10) **Keep your promises** once you get a pet. Give your animal as much love and care as possible, because they need lots of that. Then have tons of fun together!

Daring Dogs

Pros: Dogs love their owners, and your dog will quickly become one of your best friends for life. Smaller dogs are a good choice if you want one to sit on your lap. Larger dogs are good if you want a watchdog or a dog to walk you around the neighborhood. I like mutts because they are a mix of different breeds of dogs, and usually they are very good-tempered. Purebred dogs are also nice, because you can choose exactly the type of dog you want. There are many good books about purebred dogs that can help you choose the right kind of dog for you, depending on your lifestyle.

Cons: A dog is a big commitment because it has to be trained and requires lots of time, energy, and space. You may not know this, but dogs are "pack animals"—in the wild they live together in packs. This means that dogs are much happier living inside the house with you (their new pack). This is definitely something to think about before you get a dog. Don't ever keep a dog outside if you live in a place that has hot summers or cold winters.

If you decide to get a dog, you will have to help train the dog because you don't want it ruining your things. Puppies are like young children who don't know that it is not okay to chew everything up. You have to be patient and work with the puppy to teach it what is right and wrong. This usually will take a long time and you will need a lot of patience. If you want help training your dog, you can take your dog to school, or you can get a helpful book.

Finding The Right Dog
There are lots of ways to find your perfect dog.
- Go to dog shows to meet private breeders.
- Maybe you know someone whose dog is having puppies.
- Look in the classified ads in the newspaper to find dogs for sale.

If you don't want to spend a lot of money, you can get a dog from a local rescue club. These clubs find homes for dogs that cannot be kept by their owners any more. You can find rescue clubs in your area for a particular breed by contacting your local humane society.

I don't recommend getting a dog from a pet store because oftentimes they get the puppies from breeders who don't take good care of them. The puppies are also more likely to be sick.

The Humane Society

I think the best place to get a dog is from the local humane society or animal shelter. You can find purebred dogs and mutts there and you will be saving a little lost dog who badly needs a good home. In addition to dogs, the humane society also has cats, hamsters, rats, guinea pigs, ducks, geese, and rabbits for adoption! For general information call the American Humane Association at 1-800-227-4645. To find the closest humane society to you, look in your phone book.

Cuddly Cats

Pros: Cats usually don't require as much time as dogs because they are more independent. However, they still need food, water, and a clean litter box. If you want your cat to be more social with people, then you need to handle it a lot when it is a kitten. Cats are nice to have around because they are fun to play with and hold. A happy cat purrs, which can be a nice, relaxing sound after a long day.

Cons: Like dogs, your cat will be healthier and happier if you can keep it indoors. But if your cat has to be an outdoor cat, then you need to spay or neuter your cat so it can't add more kittens to the world. Also, did you know that outside cats kill thousands of endangered birds every year? If you put a small bell on your cat, it will be less likely to kill birds because they will hear the cat coming.

Gorgeous Guinea Pigs

If you don't think a dog or a cat is right for you then maybe a guinea pig, rabbit, or other small rodent would be a good choice. These animals don't require as much time, and they don't take up a lot of space. They only need space enough for a cage with a water bottle and a food bowl.

It's nice to have a guinea pig because you can hold it on your lap and you can teach it tricks. For example, my guinea pig Humbug knows that when I click my tongue she will get a treat. When she hears me click my tongue she starts to squeak and comes looking for her treat. This is a good trick to teach a guinea pig because if it ever gets lost in your room, you can click your tongue and it will squeak and come to find its treat.

Guinea pigs need to have their cage cleaned once or twice a week and their nails clipped every couple of months. Some people prefer hamsters, mice, rabbits, gerbils, or rats, and all these small animals can be bought at a pet shop or found at your local humane society.

Leapin' Lizards, Frogs, And Snakes

Lizards, frogs, and snakes are probably the easiest pets to care for. These pets need a small aquarium-like container that has branches, dirt and plants in it. They need water sprayed daily on the plants like dew for them to drink. They also need live crickets, flies, or other insects for them to eat (you can buy these at pet stores). Chameleons are interesting animals to watch because they change colors! If you want a really cuddly pet, though, this probably isn't the best choice. They are really more for watching.

Decisions, Decisions

Choosing the right kind of pet is an important decision. You have to know how much time your pet will need each day and whether you are willing to give it that time. You have to decide how much money and space you are willing to commit to the care of your pet. There is a very wide range! For instance, an Irish Wolfhound can cost up to $25.00 per week to feed and it grows to be the size of a small pony! A chameleon takes up a small amount of space in your room and can be fed for less than $1.00 per week.

When choosing a pet, don't forget to find out about the life span of that animal. Dogs and cats can live up to 15 or 20 years, but a guinea pig may only live 3 to 7 years. When choosing a pet you need to remember that you will be responsible for its whole life. If for any reason you can no longer take care of your pet, then it's your job to find it a new home where it will be happy.

Pets are good to have because they are companions that will always love you if you treat them correctly. Choose your pet wisely, treat it with care, and it will be your best friend for life!

Top Ten Ways To Welcome Your New Pet Home

Nicole Norton, age 11

✤ Dream: *to be a vet and the vice president of the USA*

It is a really exciting moment when you bring your new pet home. You can expect lots of smiles and hard work. Here is everything you need to know to be ready for the big day!

1) Remember that when you first get a pet it will be scared because it is going to a new place. Make sure you make it feel comfortable and wanted.

2) Pay attention to what your pet wants. It may be tired and may need to rest after it checks out the new place.

3) Before your pet comes home, call your vet and ask about the pet laws in your state. If you get a dog or cat, you will want to get it registered in case it gets lost.

4) Ask everyone in the house to be very careful when they open the front door so your new pet doesn't escape.

5) Make sure you have the basic supplies such as food, toys, a food dish, and maybe a cage. If you get a dog or cat, you need a collar, pooper scooper, leash, and/or a litter box.

6) You should prepare a special section in your house for the pet so it can sleep and relax. It will be their own place.

7) Just like babies, pets need schedules. They like to be fed and walked at the same time every day. Before your pet comes, figure out when you are going to do what.

8) Before your new pet goes to sleep, play with it. That way it will burn energy and sleep better during that first night.

9) Make sure you have a special blanket that is just for your pet to curl up in. A night light will also help it sleep.

10) Discuss all the rules with everyone in your family, so everyone is doing the same thing!

Final Thoughts

Having a pet is a lot of responsibility and hard work, but a pet also cheers you up and makes you laugh. So love your pet and it will love you, too!

Overcoming Shyness

Julia Halprin Jackson, age 13

✂ Hobbies: *reading, writing, soccer, swimming, working in my garden* ☹ Pet peeve: *when people act superior*
📖 Hero: *my mom* ❀ Dream: *to become a successful author and make a difference*

Timid Talk

For most girls, making an impression is really important. Everyone wants to be thought of as nice, friendly, and smart. I am a 13-year-old girl who has fought shyness for, well, 13 years. I wrote this chapter to let girls know that if you want to, you have the power to become an outgoing person who is not afraid to show her true self.

My Battle Against Shyness

I have been shy all my life. When I was really little, I had a hard time smiling in public. When I went to the store with my mom, I hid behind her so I wouldn't have to talk to her friends. One of my friends I have known since pre-school, says she was afraid of me for a long time because I always looked like I was mad at her.

When I was young, people thought that being shy was cute and they figured it would wear off. But for me, shyness didn't just disappear—I had to work at it.

As I grew older, I was still very shy and people would make comments like, "Where's your smile?" Sometimes adults mimicked me with exaggerated frowns. This always made me mad and upset. Our former rabbi would constantly say things like, "Oops! Did I make you blush?" which made me even more shy. Kids at school would also tease me about my shyness. Because I was quiet and shy, a lot of people got the impression that I was angry and pessimistic.

From Bashful To Bold

By fifth grade I realized that I needed and wanted to change. But I didn't just change overnight—I started with little steps. First, I tried hard to smile more at people I saw. I tried to talk more often and I volunteered to do things. It happened slowly, but I worked hard to socialize more and more. People began to talk to me more often. I realized that many of the people who had misunderstood my shyness were not trying to hurt my feelings.

My perspective on life changed for the better and I could tell people were beginning to think of me as a nice and friendly person. I have traveled on stormy seas, but at last the sun is shining brightly. If you are shy too and you want to change, then here is some advice that really helped me. Read on!

Use Your Smile

Do you avoid looking at people? Try looking people in the eye and smiling at everything and everyone you meet. Even though it might feel weird smiling at say, a tree frog, it is good practice and makes your overall attitude cheerier. The more you smile, the more people will begin to realize what a friendly, outgoing person you really are, even if they don't know you.

Get Involved

Are you often alone? Try getting more involved. It is a good idea to join clubs, sports teams, or groups. If you are very busy and don't have time for anything else, just do small things like helping in class by passing out papers, or just casually chatting with the people around you. The more time you spend with people, the more comfortable you will become, and it will be easier and easier for you to get to know people and overcome your shyness.

Talk  It Out

Do you get tongue-tied talking to people? Take every chance to practice conversation. Practice with your family or even stuffed animals. If you are bored waiting for a school bus, turn to the person beside you and ask them how they are doing. If there is a break during school, talk to a classmate about their projects and compare ideas. If you have the power to strike up a friendly conversation with anyone you want, you have the power to do almost anything!

No Big Deal

Do you assume other people don't like you? I have noticed that a big factor in being shy is misunderstanding the actions of others. If you are smiling at your friend and she is glowering into the distance, you might automatically think that she is mad at you. But it could be that she got a D on a math test, or that she got in a fight with her mom last night, or that her brand new scrunchy was ruined in the rain. It could be anything, so sometimes it is better just to relax and assume that the situation doesn't involve you at all. It probably doesn't.

One of my good friends is known to daydream or stare stonily into the distance. For a long time when she did this I thought she was really mad at me. Finally I realized that she just tends to ponder things over, and whatever she's thinking about has nothing to do with me.

Express Yourself

Do you hide your opinions in public? We shy people often have very strong ideas and opinions, but we feel insecure about showing our true selves for fear of being teased. If you have this problem, try to show your true colors; if people make fun of you, that's their problem. If you have enough courage to stand up for what you believe in, even when people disagree with you, they will eventually admire you for it. I can understand that you may feel awkward; it is a very normal thing. Just remember that standing up for yourself will make you feel stronger and it will make your opinions and ideas stronger, too. You are unique and talented in your own way, so be proud to be you!

New Girl In Town

Are you mystified about how to make new friends? When a new girl (or boy) moves into your school or neighborhood, it is the perfect chance to practice your friendliness! She will want to make new friends, but may also be shy. If you don't feel comfortable starting up a conversation, try smiling at her whenever you see her. Wave at her, figure out how to eat with her at lunch, ask her about homework, study together, and eventually she will be comfortable with you. By that time, you will be on your way to a successful friendship.

The True Test: In Front Of Everyone

Does speaking in public make you want to die? For people who are shy, class presentations can be pure torture! If your teacher recently assigned an oral report, you better read on! It can be really scary to talk in front of a lot of people. The most important thing is to practice, practice, practice. Just like anything else, you will feel more comfortable if you read your report in front of your parents and friends first. Work on speaking your words clearly and slowly. It's okay if you stumble over a few words; everybody does that.

Remember that everyone is nervous when they do something new. You are no exception. When you are in front of the class, try to relax. It really helps me to focus on what I am saying, instead of everyone looking at me. You could even try focusing on one person in your class (maybe a friend or at least someone you like) and pretend that you're speaking just to them.

Feeling uncomfortable in front of others isn't limited to class presentations, though. When you are around many people you don't know, it is common to feel like everyone is staring at you. This may happen to you in the cafeteria, on the bus, or during school assemblies. Everyone has a different way of handling situations like this, but I suggest that you try to ignore what is going on around you and look for a friendly face. Usually no one is really staring at you, so you don't have to worry.

Believe It Or Not—Everyone Is Shy

Even though it might not seem to be true, everyone is shy or gets embarrassed sometimes. Some people may hide it better than others, but we are all afraid of being rejected. So before you envy the class clown who always looks comfortable, remember that even they are afraid of getting their feelings hurt. For instance, a good friend of mine is a really outgoing and enthusiastic person. She is not the type of person you'd expect to be shy *at all*. But when I asked her about how she felt, I was really surprised when she told me that she often feels shy inside, too.

And hey, there's nothing wrong with being shy. Lots of cool, famous people were shy—like Albert Einstein and Michael Jordan. It's only a problem if it bothers you. You just need to work on it, like anything else. And once you are more outgoing, when you see someone else who is shy, be friendly and kind to them. Now go out there and HAVE SOME FUN (and it doesn't have to be loud or in front of people)!

Do You Want To
Be An Author, Too?
Here's Your Chance

Beyond Words Publishing will be compiling more *Girls Know Best* collections, and they are looking for more fantastic girl writers RIGHT NOW! If you are 6 to 16 years old and have a great chapter idea that isn't already in this book (or is different in some way), you could be one of the next girl authors. Here are the rules:

1. Your chapter idea can be from you alone, or you can work together with your sister(s) or best friend(s). (They also have to be 6 to 16 years old.)

2. Your chapter idea should be fun, unique, useful advice or activities for girls. It should also include one paragraph telling why you chose to write about that topic or how you got your idea and why it's important or (if it's an activity) fun to you.

3. Send 2-3 pages of your chapter idea (typed or clearly handwritten), a self-addressed stamped envelope (to return your chapter to you), and the "*Girls Know Best* Potential Author Questionnaire" (photocopied from the next page and filled out) to:

> Girl Writer Contest
> Beyond Words Publishing, Inc.
> 20827 N.W. Cornell Road, Suite 500
> Hillsboro, Oregon 97124-9808

4. You can also send a photo (any photo is fine) of yourself, if you want to, but a photo is optional.

Believe in yourself • Go for your dreams

Girls Know Best
Potential Author Questionnaire

PLEASE DO NOT WRITE IN THIS BOOK! Photocopy this page and fill out your information in the spaces provided. Handwritten is fine. If you can't think of an answer to something, it's okay to leave it blank. Mail your completed questionnaire with your chapter idea to Beyond Words Publishing, Inc.

Name _____ **Age** _____

Address _____

City _____ **State** _____ **Zip Code** _____

Phone Number (___) _____ (to call you if you win. Beyond Words Publishing will not call you for any other reason.)

Your hobbies:

Your favorite subject or class in school:

Your favorite writer and/or book:

Your biggest pet peeve:

Your hero or role model:

Something that makes you unique:

Your dream:

Anything else you want to say:

Glossary

advocating: publicly supporting, or showing favor toward, someone or something, usually by speaking or writing about it to gain the support of others.

anxiety: a painfully fearful state of uneasiness or worry about something expected to happen in the future.

charismatic: having qualities that are particularly appealing and which establish a special popularity with friends and followers who are very loyal and supportive.

collages: artwork formed by arranging various scraps of materials, such as magazine pictures, fabric, photographs, newspaper, and wood, and gluing them onto a surface.

concoctions: the various results of mixing together different ingredients or raw materials, such as in cooking.

contraptions: gadgets or unusual pieces of equipment, such as tools or machines, that were invented for special uses in clever or artistic ways.

forlorn: hopelessly lonely; feeling left out or deserted.

genetic: passed on or developed through heredity.

glowering: looking extremely angry; scowling.

immigrants: people who arrive in a foreign country intending to stay permanently.

incubation: the process of developing or growing in an environment that is kept safe, warm, and comfortable.

intimidated: having feelings of fear or inferiority caused by the words or actions of a person or group or by an extremely difficult situation.

introspective: able to look inside yourself to examine your own thoughts and feelings.

intuition: knowledge or feelings that come from inside oneself without any clear reasoning.

itinerary: a planned route to get from one place to another; a travel plan.

negotiate: to discuss an argument or a difference of opinion in order to come to an agreement or a compromise.

perspective: the particular way a person sees or understands a situation based on his or her knowledge or background; point of view.

privileged: having special rights or advantages not common for everybody.

procrastinated: purposely put off, usually for no good reason, doing something that needs to be done.

waifs: homeless people, especially children, who do not have a family or friends.

More Books to Read

101 Things to Do on the Internet. Mark Wallace, ed. (Educational Development Center)

Best Friends: A Special Book of True Friendship. Poppy Bloom (Element Books)

Color Crazy: A Guide to Understanding the Colors in Your Life. Lori Reid (Element Books)

Emotional Ups and Downs. Good Health Guides (series). Enid Fisher (Gareth Stevens)

Feeling Shy. Exploring Emotions (series). Althea Braithwaite (Gareth Stevens)

The Junior High Survival Manual. Katrina L. Cassel (Concordia)

People with Disabilities. What Do You Know About (series). Pete Sanders and Steve Myers (Copper Beech).

A Pet or Not? What a Pet (series). Alvin Silverstein, *et al* (TFC)

Super Slumber Parties. Brooks Whitney (Pleasant Company)

Sweet Dreamer: A Guide to Understanding Your Dreams. Lori Reid and Preston Bradley (Element Books)

What on Earth Do You Do When Someone Dies? Trevor Romain and Elizabeth Verdick (Free Spirit)

Videos

Friends First (series). (United Learning, Inc.)

The Internet Show. (PBS Home Video)

Peer Pressure. (Schlessinger Media)

Sally at Thirteen: Daydreams and Nightmares. (AGC Educational Media)

Web Sites

Girl tech. (www.girltech.com)

Girls' Place. (www.girlsplace.com)

The InSite. (talkcity.com/theinsite)

A Peace of Paper. (www.worldkids.net/clubs/apop)

Teen Voices online. (www.teenvoices.com)

To find additional Web sites, use a reliable search engine with one or more of the following keywords: *blues, candy, death, disabilities, dreams, friendship, Internet, jobs, peer pressure, pets, poetry, relationships, self-esteem, shyness, slumber parties, toys.*

Index